Detour

Steve April

Detour
 Printed in the U.S.A.
c/o POB 4475
Mountain View, Ca 94040-0331
Second Printing
ISBN 978-0-9744686-8-6
A Barberry Book

to Maxine, who makes me wonder

Also by Steve April

Poetry

Poet In California
The Einstein Club
The Sunflower
Scenes From Law School
Birds In America

5 Short Stories

Contents

PART 1

1

R. had been feeling odd since midday. He reached for the car keys, and Kimberly withdrew them. R. turned, regarded the evening sky, and giggled. Kimberly was toying and he had to go see off Ivan and Lisa.

R. leaned, waiting, tensed yet fluid, a thin, wiry figure in a door.

Kimberly handed R. the keys, gazed a moment in the area of his biceps, smiled, R. imagined, as Mona Lisa, and enunciated at the level of a whisper, "see you later." The words seemed to form an intoxicating cloud around and about him.

"Sure, yeah," R. replied to the shut door, and headed off to the airport.

R. gunned the car out of the driveway in a cloud of dust, and sped along, the moon was an orange fist above.

He was in a hopeful mood. "I'm going to commune with her tonight, I can feel it. Yes, the pendulum's swung. Kimberly's going to show me love has no better emissary than she. And to think it's this way because of Ariane perhaps, at the party the other night. I guess no one gets hurt by ardent love, I can't say it hurts me."

One minute off, a mile or so away, came George and Jersey, destination Kimberly's.

Encased in mustache and aviator glasses, George was in law school. He'd been Kimberly's friend for years, since freshmen together in high school. He exuded a species of arrogant craft and cleverness. R. disliked him and the feeling was mutual. Jersey was a pharmacology student, and Ariane's lover. Good-willed, quiet, clumsy, he held in relation to George the position a butler will hold to his master; they were together frequently and George dominated.

"God," George was complaining. "These bumps are outrageous. Look at that blind curve. What a lawsuit against the county in the making."

"Why do you call him Rodney Hot-Shot, because he's such a nothing?" Jersey interrupted. "I've rarely seen feelings like the kind you have for him, George. You call him that because he's a loser, a nothing, right?" Jersey concluded, mouth open, panting as a puppy will.

"No," replied George in typically swillish fashion, at least where R. was concerned. "It's because he kissed your girlfriend. Ha ha. Jersey, if dodos could fly you'd be an astronaut."

"Aw George."

R. whistled as he drove the well-used '99 Chevy.

The road on which the two cars approached required strenuous little detours, it was cracked, broken up, under construction.

As R. drove through the night he hummed. ""Blame it on the moon," R. swore softly through his teeth at the moon over the open fields as he whizzed along.

As George and Jersey passed him in the night, Jersey exclaimed, "hey, isn't that Kimberly's car?" George nodded. "Yes," George muttered, suddenly excited, "and this is our chance, our big chance while he's gone to set her straight. He's turned her practically into a slave after all, anyone can see it. We must break his hold on her, we must demonstrate to her sharply and clearly how vicious, how cruel, and really mean-hearted he is. For Kimberly's own good."

Jersey nodded halfheartedly.

"You'll help me, right?" George turned to him. "I hope I can depend on you for after all dear friend, you found him at the party in the closet making out with Ariane, and Ariane's your girl friend."

"But you're doing it because you want Kimberly," Jersey blurted.

"Jersey," George practically spit between clenched teeth. "Sometimes…"

"Gee, I'm coming, aren't I?" Jersey whimpered plaintively. "Let's be friends George."

As R.'s tail lights receded, once more they fell silent.

"Why do you have to, I wish you wouldn't, I didn't think it would happen, and if you don't come back I don't know," R. protested. "There you go off to distant places, oxcarts on dusty streets, caravans, floating markets, you're so lucky…"

"What a feigned protest, too late. 'Med school, straightening out, Kimberly.' Why I wouldn't have believed it if I hadn't heard it with my own ears," responded Ivan.

"Yah, in a sense, it's you who are betraying, or deserting us," Lisa insisted, looking reproachful.

"Well, nevertheless, wherever you go there you are, wherever I go, there I am," replied R. "You're going off, you're the ones flying free, going on a great adventure, and I'll be here, here in this place, soon to be a student, that is to say, unhappy. I'll be here so goodbye, I can't stand it, wish me luck in my new career, and when you get back call…"

They said their goodbyes and R. drove off. He would miss them.

Walking back to the car, the night was cooler, and clearer. Well, there were some positive aspects. "Now to Kimberly and love," he exclaimed, at the toll booth, paying his ticket, and was off. Little did he realize what was approaching.

Who was he? R. was a curious one; a strong, weak, outspoken, quiet piece of incendiary turmoil. Progressing as he did through ferment, conflict, contradiction, mercurial seemed to be his rising star. It drove Kimberly up the wall, and down the other side. There was a charisma, a magnetism, that attracted and drew friends close, and people in general would often give him a double glance. However, there was a wildness, an excitement, that bordered on inconstancy, and caused many to hesitate, from the beginning. At this point he was worried. He had reason to be. A mood was upon him he recognized with an emotion akin to dread, as brother to a mood eight months before, which, quite against his conscious will, hurled him towards episodes of drunkenness, and excess among his social relations.

He had recovered, he found, with praiseworthy will and determination, the desire to change and felt a new need for stability, for surety. Due to Kimberly's love, Dr. Pike's support, and that her father would feel like mentoring him, Ivan and Lisa's friendship, he had drawn himself from the insidious, self-destructive snare. Amazingly, and he was glad, yes. His heart leaped. He'd as Dr. Pike suggested "straightened himself out," and applied to a top notch med school, and on the basis of a brilliant, if occasionally erratic school career, with a few leaves, had been accepted. He was going to go to school, turn over a new leaf, start over, and put behind these desultory episodes. Times were tough. He could not afford to slide. He could no longer go on being supportive of his own irresponsibility. Yet here this state arose again.

At the party she stormed out, she sensed his distance through his antics. She hopped into her car and drove home. Later, R. downplayed and backpedaled, but didn't believe it. Why did he go into that closet with Ariane? Well, a few drinks will do that, he could say easily. However, lately he noticed his back muscle stiffen, like a cat, amid her conservative confines, and expectations, that were not conservative at all, but healthy and practical. The razor's edge between freedom and slavery is walked by love. Was he seeing her parents in her? However, he wanted that arm-chair, a fireplace in the evening, diplomas on the wall. Perhaps he was spooked. George and Jersey, he was allergic to them. Perhaps that was connected to his little escapade.

As R. turned, leaving the airport, having no Ivan or Lisa as middle ground, he felt foreboding. He'd miss them terribly. Though only for three or four months, R. turned to problems; two less friends, both dear; a career he perhaps didn't want; "significant other" problems; and a nature, seemingly in equilibrium only in conflict, contradiction, that seemed to drive him to excesses he later most of all came to question.

As he drove foreboding increased. He saw, felt a net come down, enfold, and lift his car.

Time was running out.

About three miles away, George and Jersey made the turn into the Pike residence. It had been a rainy summer; it was beginning to drizzle.

George, as we have seen, smarting from the turn Kimberly had made from him, in the direction of R., was determined to make her miserable. Vanity in hand with affection for Kimberly drove him, she had ruffled his feathers in a major way.

As George and Jersey's insinuations grew more and more insulting and unpalatable, Kimberly bridled. Red as a beet, she exclaimed, "well, so what if he did make out with Ariane, big deal. We've had it out. We've been through it. I understand it. And you don't. He wanted to 'shake things up' and you must admit he succeeded. I understand you hate him but he's mine. I'm sorry Jersey, since you and Ariane are together, but I guess it goes to show she's got a mind of her own, and a view her own. He kissed her a few times in the closet, after a few drinks, the sky's not falling, the sun will rise tomorrow.

I consider the matter finished. I think also, you're both rather despicable to come here behind his back when he's not here to defend himself, and stir up trouble.

Really, what a pair of cowards."

And she laughed, if painfully.

"You're being stupid Kimberly, you're letting yourself in for a fall, you'll be sorry later," Geroge intoned nastily.

"Get out of my house," Kimbery stood and pointed. "The day of the jackals. Don't come back. Ever." She burned with anger and misery.

The road was full of little detours and he was distracted.

Somewhere a jet, Ivan and Lisa's, streaked above, a silver sliver.

Whether it was the moon, the beers, the detours, and construction, the unfamiliar stretch of road, I'm going to skip over the details of the crash. Suffice it to say the accident happened, the moment came. R. sensed a net come down, enfold, lift, and hurtle. He was at the wheel but not in control. He perhaps gave vent to words such as, "Left, gone! And I've not told them anything! I am fortune's fat in the fire."

And Kimberly was wondering, "where could he be? That scoundrel. After I defend him, he goes and stays out late, after pledging to return immediately."

Kimberly descended the stairs to the living room and her parents. "Where could he be? I just can't understand him being out so late. Why doesn't he come back already? Given that he likes to stay out late but there's nowhere around here to go unless he's found one," she was complaining theatrically.

Her parents continued with the tv and paper.

"He'll be back," her father, on automatic pilot,

assured her. "My daughter is so vulnerable," he was musing poignantly. "I hope he deserves her."

"I want him so badly."

"Why?" inquired her father.

"To rub my back," Kimberly answered immediately, saucily.

Mrs. Pike looked up, over the paper, blushing a bit.

"Look Kimberly, you're shocking your mother," teased Dr. Pike, cruising on the remote. So many channels, but nothing much to see.

"I want him so badly," Kimberly repeated, for the second time. "If he's messed up my car, he'll pay," she threatened.

She sat, bit her scarf, and waited.

At 12:43 a.m. the car and R. cracked up. He'd mentioned to Kimberly only that he needed to borrow it, that he was seeing off his friends; did not mention them by name.

At 2:07 a.m. the crack up was spotted by a passing motorist. He yelled down, and receiving no answer, called for help from a gas station. He was not carrying a cell phone. At 2:26 the call came in and at 2:32 an ambulance was dispatched. Sam, the driver, and Joe, in back, had their problems. Finally they found the wreck. The motorist had confused the routes, and they'd made a wrong turn, to boot. "A bad one," Joe shouted, returning.

In the early hours on a morning in June in the town of K---, a phone rang in the Pike residence. Kimberly answered. The hospital informed her that her friend R. was in a crash, and in critical condition in the intensive care ward. Kimberly woke her parents, and they sped down, she, a habitual gesture, biting her scarf.

"Kimberly, don't bite your scarf," her mother admonished, straining, in an odd way, to ease the tension.

Dr. Fairchild met them at the nurse's desk. Dr. Fairchild presented a strong, jutting chin, flared nostrils, a sensual mouth, with full lips, and wavy, silver hair. He had a dimple on his chin. His shoulders were broad, his body athletic and powerful. The only feature that marred his Hollywood good looks was a slightly florid complexion. Perhaps too many years playing golf or tennis at the club on the weekends. Though in his early 50s, he seemed younger.

He stood cadaverous, portentous, and strode forward and shook hands with Dr. Pike, an acquaintance, and informed them succinctly, "He's lucky to be alive. Injuries extensive. Broken ribs. Neck pulled. Concussions, and the like. Recovery will be painful and slow."

"Dear R.,

Gotta tell you, it's great being away from America. All the pressure's off.

No money-obsessed, aggressive, reductive dildos that enter your home through tv, here we drift with the sea breezes, move languidly, when we want to, go on hikes up a mountain, take in the scenery.

"The views are refreshing, the natives are friendly, here in Thailand hee hee.

Our tour guide, Carl, adopted us, hangs with us, savvy about places to go, things to see. The streets bustle in the cities. The hostels are okay. Cockroaches big as your hand, rusty bed springs, sagging mattress, bad for the back. Lisa started feeling dizzy the other day, went to the clinic, turns out a cockroach crawled into her ear, and started an infection, she's taking antibiotics.

"Don't mean to quibble. Theirs is an ancient culture that values their relation with nature, and peace of mind. The food's tasty. Usually, on top of the cash register, smiles a Buddha, a puffy, golden Buddha, smiling beautifically.

"Life is good!

au revoir,

Ivan

p.s.

Lisa sends her love to you and Kimberly."

Fairly, Connecticut is a small town nestled in the foothills, an affluent suburb, boasting spacious Mediterranean style homes, or split level residences with handsome brick fronts and stonework around the doorways, or pillars and facades.

In the Revolutionary War, the town was marched on by the British, on their way to Boston. George Washington stayed nearby, with his army, on his way to Valley Forge.

There were parks, shopping malls, a school system that is well funded, with rising property taxes, the affluent post WW2 years, into the 70s, and becomes a major draw for young professionals, working in Manhattan, starting a family. Dr. Pike made the ride as a young man, and learned much listening to audio books, on the long commute home. Dr. Pike's affection for and appreciation of the arts sprang from these sessions, that saved him countless hours of boredom, and filled his car with joy and intelligence. Classical CDs, and jazz, also contributed to his winding-down, after a long day at the hospital.

Having grown up in the 60s, and being naturally hardworking, conservative, and upbeat, few things mattered more to him than his daughter's happiness. She was the jewel in the crown, the apple of his eye. She was the light of his life.

Stone crouching, poured concrete gargoyles, subdivided rectangles in an underground labyrinth with cars, under withering, glaring florescent lights, Dr. Pike strode oblivious, secure in his routine.

Later that afternoon, Dr. Pike walked to his car in the underground university parking lot. First day of classes, a few kids recovering from hangovers, the new faces, the fresh, eager looks and expectations. He never got over the optimism of youth. "Their spirits soar affirmatively at the start of a new enterprise," he mumbled. "Like they're on a rocket ship. New adventures, new enterprises. Boldly go where no one has gone before."

Amid the concrete gargoyles, subdivided rectangles in an underground labyrinth with cars, under glaring florescent lights, Dr. Pike strode, secure in his routine.

"They're breaking through the atmospheric fires, and the gravity that presses down on them, the hero with a thousand faces, feeling the burn on a new journey, working to be free from childish ways, constraints, from awkward immaturity, from innocence. They're coming of age."

He felt a little slip in his chest, and a sudden pressure,

a heaviness. He felt sweaty suddenly. His heart began beating faster. Unlocking his car door, he collapsed to the ground. Fortunately, a nearby student witnessed his collapse and ran over, turning over his crumpled form, barely responsive. "Call 911," the doctor murmured.

"Oh Jesus, not Daddy," Kimberly screamed when her mother called, and told her the news.

"He's okay. They want to keep him under observation, but he's okay. It could have been much worse."

"Daddy should know better, he refuses to give up his ice cream. A whole quart's gone after a day or two, and you and I and R. don't touch it."

"That's his comfort food," replied her mother. "I know. He's in his early 60s. He works too hard."

"He should take better care of himself," Kimberly roared.

Kimberly's fury turned to stone-cold dread, when she hung up the phone.

What would she do without her father to console her, counsel her, guide her, be there for her? "You've been splendid to R.," Kimberly praised him, and petted his hand in the hospital room.

The room was spacious, his insurance was optimal. The professor's union took care of that. Health care was a substantial perk, to draw top-tier talent to the school, like Dr. Pike.

"Doctor says a day or two observation, tests reveal your father had a mild stroke," a pretty Asian nurse informed her in the hall. "No permanent damage so far noted."

"So far noted," Kimberly screamed, in the hall.

"I don't know, it takes time," the nurse responded. "Ask the doctor.

"Your dad's okay, don't worry."

"Sorry to hear about your father, Kimberly. Oh, my God. I feel guilty. I'm going to be needing my space for awhile. Be spending time over at my apartment. Have much research to do, esoteric studies. Also, could I borrow $5,000?"

"A two-fer," thought Kimberly, desperately. But she didn't want to lose him. She would have married him, if he would ask.

"What for, may I inquire?" responded Kimberly.

"A private eye," said R. "I have a feeling, a feeling deep inside, like the song goes."

2

March Nesmith, R. liked the ring of that, and dialed the number from the google search. R. explained the broad outlines of his mission and concerns, and they agreed to meet at a Peet's coffee shop in a nearby town, far enough from Kimberly's house to afford R. a comfort zone.

"You look like Serpico, with the black cap," March observed as they were sitting down.

"Never seen that," said R.

"Do you receive a ribbing, most folks would assume March is a girl's name," R. inquired, after a few familiarities.

They were sitting at a little table, looking out on a breezy autumn day, leaves piling on the lawn outside, but a pleasing Schubert piece playing over the sound system, with a few scattered afternoon coffee fiends. They were glued to their computers.

"Oh whatever," March said. "The androgyny in me perhaps," he quipped, a burly, broad shouldered guy with a bull neck and a touch of sag, and black glasses.

"I relate to that," quipped R.

"Well, I'm a veteran. Got the moniker when we

moved on the double, I was in charge of supplies, on our march."

"I served in Iraq," R. responded. "Got out alive anyway."

They exchanged a few stories about their squadrons, platoon leaders, locales.

R. cut to the chase. "Bad car accident. Smelled alcohol on the doctor's breath when he prepped me for surgery, though I was pretty out-of-it. Have a bad feeling about the guy. Also, received vague threats, maybe a bit paranoid."

"And?"

"Want to run a background check on the doctor, Dr. Fairchild. Who is he, where did he come from, what's his financial situation, does he have a family? Perhaps most importantly, his medical side, any history of complaints, and all the details, names, places, dates, concerning the complaints. If there are any. The text of them would be very helpful, and the names and the addresses of the complaining parties."

"A fair amount of work," March ruminated. March plopped a bag of pistachios on the table, and unshelled a few, poured a few out. "Want some? Good source of protein, or for cardio, and won't add fat like peanuts." He placed the shells in his half-empty coffee cup.

R. popped one in his mouth, and they quickly came to terms on a retainer and a report schedule.

Walking out to the car R. exclaimed, "I heard a couple people talking about 'getting rid' of someone in the hospital lounge near where I was laid up, not sure if they were referring to me. Pretty sure they work there."

"If you can find out their names," advised March, "I'll run a check on them, it'll be on me."

A week later, good to his word, March slid a report across the table, while the sound system played Beethoven's 6th.

"Alright R., Richard, here's my preliminary report. Sorry to be the bearer of bad news or maybe good news, depending on your view. Regarding Dr. Fairchild. There have been 32 complaints against him, that I could find so far."

"Merde" exclaimed R. "Are you kidding me?"

"Well, maybe. No clue the substance of the complaints, other than that they were filed to the medical board in the state. Have no idea, so far, what the problem is."

"Also, you have to remember, he may be doing a lot of procedures, and he's been practicing many, many years. There are quite a few factors, like how many procedures per year he performs, what kind of patients, high risk or low risk, what kinds of procedures, high risk or low risk. Also, how many, if any go to court," he added. "It's all preliminary."

"Get more info. I need ammo," urged R.

"Will see what shakes out," said March, "in the coming weeks. Stay tuned."

"When will I hear from you next, with details?" said R. "I need details."

"Okay," said March. "By the way, the couple in the lounge, the male's a doctor, his specialty is orthopedics, the female's a retired nurse."

"Well run a background check, will you? It's important."

"So who do you like for the playoffs this season," March asked, switching gears, to R.'s consternation.

"Don't watch football, haven't in years, too many commercials," R. yawned, leaning forward.

March Nesmith's second report. "Interesting, very interesting. This brilliant surgeon may be a skank after all. Listen to this," said March. "Way back, after med school, in his intern years, Dr. Fairchild got accused of solicitation, and rape. Seems like him and a gang of fellow med students formed a club or posse, and began personal relationships with young, attractive female patients, in some cases making them an offer they could not refuse."

"English," said R.

"They offered these girls cash gifts, trips to valued destinations like Hawaii, prescription drugs, and discounted medical treatment. They would party together and do Quaaludes and have "swinger" sex apparently. I read a girl's complaint, an 18 year old at the time.

"Also, they would buy girls drinks, and slips pills in their drinks a la Bill Cosby, and have group sex, or multiple partners. The girl never knew what hit her, according to the complaint. She remembers being in his apartment, and having drinks, and she wakes up nude the next morning in Dr. Fairchild's bed, with no memory of the events the night before."

"Really," R. screamed. "Did they arrest him?" Heads turned.

"Nope," March replied. "Came out in a deposition in a civil suit, that was settled privately between Dr.

Fairchild and Ms. X., who remains anonymous.

"The D.A. couldn't bring charges, the girl did not want to testify. It's in an obscure, mislabelled cardbox box, over at the State Medical Board building, under False Pretenses. Much redacted. Don't ask why, comes with the territory."

"Well, what a bombshell," R. exclaimed urgently.

"Oh yeah, one more problem, "March continued. "This happened over 25 years ago, and there's no trace of this gal anywhere and I checked."

"What year?"

"1990."

"What state?"

"Texas. Where he did his intern and residency. Houston area. Everything's bigger in Texas, they say. Laugh Out Loud."

"Not far from where I was born," remarked R. "Curiouser and curiouser."

"Oh hell, what now?" R. demanded, and wondered.

"Well, I did additional research on the nature, and temperature, of those complaints. Most were for medical malpractice."

"Any go to trial?"

"A few."

"Sounds like, 'Yo, problem.' His license still intact?"

"The State Medical Board, are you kidding? No national register. The white wall of silence. They don't take kindly to strangers, in these here parts. They're on the doctor's side against the ambulence chasers, except in clear cut cases of –well, murder—intentional, malicious acts."

"Oh, hell," said R.

"Ever hear of the myth of Sissyphus, who rolls the rock up the hill, only to have it roll down again, that's what you're up against, if you go against the Board and the doctor."

"Oh hell, oh hell. Think March, think. This could be big."

"Well maybe not, the other side is he's a well known surgeon, with a long, distinguished career. If you parse out the three procedures a day, 150 days a year, which after alittle research statistics may be typical, or maybe not, due to stats are all over the place, 450 procedures per year, over 25 years or so, don't know really, equals about 10,000 surgeries. High risk surgeries, by the way. In addition, he publishes frequently."

"So," continued March," 32 complaints or so out of 10,000 high risk patients equals less than 1%, do the math here, hmm, .32% he'll argue. And did I mention, he publishes frequently?"

"He's no good, I smelled him from a mile away," R. insisted vehemently.

"Yeah, maybe," replied March. "Also, a frequent issue in such cases is predators often have a target class. Maybe he's got antipathy for a young stud like yourself, with a gorgeous, pretty girlfriend. Remember O.J. and Ron Goldman?"

"O.J. and Ron Goldman? Nah, Nicole was O.J.'s ex, he was jealous as hell, Ron Goldman was incidental. Dr. Fairchild's spent a few minutes with Kimberly in the lounge, after the crash, while Kimberly waited for me."

"Well, you know the saying, jealousy, 'the green eyed beast that mocks the meat it feeds on.' He may be a perv."

"Pure speculation," responded R. "We don't know."

"You're catching on kid. Spoken like a lawyer."

"Wow, this sex ring thing, bingo" R. exclaimed. "More about that. Keep digging."

"Will do," said March.

"By the way March," said R., "how do you know my girlfriend's gorgeous?"

March chuckled. "Oh, I do alittle digging, like you say. Comes with the territory. I want to know who's paying the bills."

"Daddy, I missed a couple weeks of classes, but R. is recovering. Admin will let me play catch up. After four years earning a biology degree, I'm itching to get on with my classes."

"R. is your first patient, you're doing great," her father chided and encouraged. "He's so lucky to have you. How is he doing on his road to recovery?"

"Doing fine," Kimberly replied, admiring her father's way with words. Her father did not need to know the details, given his own compromised health condition. "I was worried sick," she said, biting her lip, and catching her breath. "You know, the med school's up in the air. The doctors say his recuperation comes first, a few months of rest and relaxation, and exercise, and healthy eating, after that traumatizing horror story," Kimberly declared. "After that, we'll see. Daddy, I'm so glad you're back home. I couldn't bear it without you." Kimberly paused. "You like Richard, Daddy, don't you? Be honest."

"In a weird way, I do," replied Dr. Pike, with a sparkle in his eye. "My daughter cares about him, and she separates the wheat from the chaff."

Kimberly gave him a big hug. Tears fell from her eyes onto his face and neck. "I'm putting a lock on the freezer, Daddy. No ice cream for you."

"Who are these people we entrust with our lives?" R. wondered histrionically, in a quickie return letter to Ivan and Lisa, in Thailand.

"Do you know how many car accident fatalities occur per year in the U.S. alone? Over 37,000 people die in road crashes each year. An additional 2.2 million are injured or disabled.

"Hey Lisa, Ivan, be careful out there. Over 90% of road fatalities occur in low and middle income countries. Across the world, about 1.2 million people die in road crashes each year, an average of over 3,200 deaths per day. I'm one of the lucky ones. I'm still here. Or am I?"

Oddly, after signing off, he recalled his childhood anxieties, how forlorn and lonely for a foster kid when you're away from familiar faces. He remembered receiving a pair of pajamas, under a Christmas tree, making the night a little more bearable.

When he returned to his apartment, he realized he had to deal with the disarray. His roommate remained in Florida, so with the place to himself, the situation became a bit more bearable.

He turned on the bathroom light and looked in the mirror. A part of him realized this practice at this stage was probably destructive and hurtful. Marks on his head and face. Wounds, angry edges barely closed, healing.

His black cap would be with him awhile. His hair was a thin stubble, barely beginning to grow back, over the jagged problem areas. Torn tendons in his arms, and broken ribs hurt terribly, but they were beginning to repair. No longer dizzy, he felt more in balance.

"Clean up time" he said, though he realized he was tackling this way too early. Luckily, his cleaning supplies were stacked in the kitchen in abundance, Comet, and Pine Sol, and ergonomic soapers and sponges, a mop, a broom, a pair of heavy duty yellow gloves, and enough large trash bags to burn a barn.

They had cleaned up his act in the Army. A few in the squad called him Mr. Clean.

"Every great journey begins with a first step," he exclaimed theatrically.

His bathtub looked frightful. An hour or so later, voila, sparkling clean.

His refrigerator needed defrosting, it had been years.

"Another day," he decided. But nearly empty, no one had been there for weeks. He scrubbed the shelving, the rims, the fruit and veggie containers.

He liked the gloves, the work seemed to glide along.

Sweeping, mopping done. A thorough vacuum cleaning, for the tacky rug. Not much improvement there, but no crunching underfoot.

Would he bring Kimberly here without feeling embarrassed, ashamed? Decidedly not, but he'd be spending time here, and habitable it was.

His wooden terrace gave him pleasure, where he put out suet or peanuts, or crumbs for the birds. All kinds visited him there, bluejays, wrens, the little sparrows.

There were two nests in a copse of trees not 15 feet from his terrace railing, 20 feet in the air, on the second floor. Hummingbirds zipped by, on their errands.

"I come to this slowly, gradually, painfully," said R. to the air, "speaking for the lost, the forgotten, abused. 'Raise your glass to the hardworking people.'"

"Funny connection, in my condition. Delerium? Now I will take action in their name, with a faith that could move mountains, because this faith is much larger than me, it's a faith with no limit to height or depth, a love with no limit. What will be, what's to come, renewed, by them, like a virgin spring. Washing the earth, 'the pure ablution around earth's human shores.'"

Staying away from the computer seemed natural the first weeks after the crash, however R. began easing back into it, with alittle assist from Secret Hero aka Sinistah, who kept pestering him with texts to meet up, and go into the studio.

R. sent him back a selfie, standing on his terrace, with a couple wrens pecking nearby.

Secret Hero shot off a return pix, with a pretty gold caption, "Serpico feeding the birds." Voila, his selfie was frameable. A little black cap, all that stood between him and the abyss. Appearances were deceiving.

Just for kicks, and because there's an urge to surge, even in untoward directions, R. drove over to the mall, to run a few errands, without his cap.

He stopped in a flower and postcard shop. He wanted to send Kimberly a Van Gogh postcard.

"Mommy, look at that man," a blond kid slurping a

Pepsi, exclaimed, tugging his mother's purse. She winced, and looked over surreptitiously and looked away. "Don't talk so loud. People can hear you."

He mosied over to a men's clothing store. A salesman came up, and turned his face away immediately. "Can I help you?" "Looking for love in all the wrong places" quipped R. "Looking for jeans." The salesman directed him to a corner of the shop. Suddenly, security guards were visible.

"Sir, we're asking you to leave the store."

"Why?" R. wondered.

"Sir, follow us. Leave the store."

R. strode out the store, and one of them yelled after him, "don't scare the kids, Frankenstein."

He moseyed into a woman's clothing store, and a bubbly young lady said, "may I help you."

"Looking for something for my girlfriend?" R. exclaimed. "Maybe lacy underwear." R. understood he was being provocative, well he felt provocative.

"Victoria's Secret, we have here," she led him shyly.

"What happened to you?" she inquired suddenly.

"A car accident. Part of my therapy is going out, and pretending things are normal," R. said.

"It looks like that really hurts," she replied. "My name's Cindi." They shook hands. "My mother's going through chemo now. She's totally bald. It's hard."

"It's hard," acknowledged R. "Only browsing," he replied. "Later."

"Feeling strong now. Mojo rising. The gal at Victoria's Secret reached out to me. Gritty, and with heart," said R. aloud. "The undifferentiated man feels inferior over/

against society. Does the shoe fit?

"The undifferentiated man is compulsively jealous. Does the shoe fit? Nah, not me. If Kimberly took up with another guy , I'd be hurt but let it go, not my nature to cling.

"The undifferentiated man feels stunted in a career. The undifferentiated man cannot help but feel oppressed by the variety and multitude of choices, not having sufficiently developed root systems and nourishment in his own ground of being. Does the shoe fit? Well, when one goes through trauma, trauma becomes a part of one. I have looked into the abyss. This car accident may be the raison d'etre for a long, severe regression.

"Who knows, maybe an opportunity in a way I cannot forsee."

from R's journal. Great reserve. A long, drawn-out, hidden silence through which all convictions, opinions, dreams, motives are being passed and through which every force going into the shaping of his personality must be processed. It is a task in itself to acccumulate a great reserve, to be delicate enough for it, strong enough for it, serious enough for it, serious enough to be willing to sacrifice dependencies on societal matters, honor, regard of contemporaries, for the dark landscapes of the interior dwelling places.

The great reserve has an analogue outside the soul; it is the period in the development of a race or of geological formations, where the forces of identity are silent and still as they make huge, incredibly slow movements below the surface, unobserved, until the moment when they explode upward and outward in a going forth. Such huge, slow movements, are the underside of the occasion of greatness; the gradual coming together and building up without which explosions are impossible. (Volcanoes, tsunamis, tectonic shifts, that float new islands.)

To the individual who puts an arm's length (a hard arm's length) between him and the world he is responsive of; who sees, hears, thinks as from a distance; who lets pass the motley show-and-tell and knows what not to concern himself over; in short, the one who does not flow out, who need not speak about something to own something; who is a stillness, a container, and a vessel—to that person goes the power and explosive potential of greatness."

R. began taking walks each morning, to stay sane. His mortal soul was at stake.

from R.'s journal.

Green Is The Color

Myopia proved operative
though the woods were very green,
so dense and brown the forest floor
and plush with the unseen.

A beaver completed his little dam,
stood there in his furry coat,
between the swamp and wilderness
an architect of some note.

While blue jays in the branches
expounded in their Portuguese,

on such matters of moment,
the newsmen in the trees.

Then the sky turned crimson
and I hurried away in a rush
through the discreet, inscrutable forest
and twilight's deceptive plush.

How sturdy and admirable these beings we call trees. How alive, and sentient in their presence and their growth. Like us they grow, like us they develop, evolve from scrub to youthful sapling, to mature, assert their presence. Arguably, among the most successful organisms on the planet.

Branches branching, trunk thickening, in strength and density.

I'd climb trees, what a joy, as a kid. Like ascending on the back of a whale, or a friendly dragon. It lets us scamper over its bumps, accepts our grasping, grappling hands that grip for dear life, to the next foothold. When we get closer to the top, dare we look up? We see blue. Dare we look down, the ground, far below, and the fall to cripple or kill.

The trees sway in the breeze, the child in the tree becomes the dreamer and the dream, the dancer and the dance.

There is an eco-system, trees are the central, sturdy player. Their sap feeds birds, their leafy canopy provides a place to mate and sing and nest.

Squirrels run up and down the oak branches, carrying acorns in their little paws, or teeth. Yellow-bellied sapsuckers drill a row of holes, make little wells, that well with sap, and insects come. Build it and they will come, the saying goes!

All this rooted in a rock hurtling around the sun at about 67,000 miles per hour, and revolving on its axis at about 1,040 miles per hour.

--That is a miracle, with a cherry on top. Amid the frozen wastes of intergalactic space sans flora, only starlight to give a portent, (an omen, a glimmer) of the little oasis in the middle of nowhere.

Traveling, traversing, transpiring, within a column, refining the energy burst into nutrients and trappings, and eliminating, conveying, transmitting nutrients to their proper destinations, reaching heights, living out their destiny, ubiquitous, patient, persevering, present.

Almost omnipresent so widespread and various, so prolific, proving, approachable, so full of potential and becoming, widely spreading their seeds all over the place.

Individuality, exception, twist, anomaly there, but also uniformity, compliance, regularity, pattern, and prototype. They congregate, associate, provide in parks.

Do they know laborious strain, with might-man, do they know the hard work, painstaking, strenuous, energetic endeavors, surely they do, every day forces of entropy mass and unite to bring them down, every day they respond in stellar dignity, keeping the proverbial wolf from the door. That they provide us shade and pleasure, part of their allure and charm.

Exterior, outward, friendly, inviting. Widening, enlarging, lengthening, promulgating, into expanse and stretch, size, proportion, strength, bestowing oxygen, their unique gift, via photosynthesis.

Yes, even though the birdsong is burnished in my brain, the song of larks in the morning seems fresh and new.

There must be a primordial receptor in me, in all of us probably, to intake and assimilate the bird song, the trees swaying lightly in the breeze, the scent of flowers, the sunlight in the trees.

There was a birth going on, a forest walk. There were new sensations, new paths, a walker forced to choose, and emerging, new horizons. Far from

'Rush in boy, punch your number
to earn your dosh,
for another dreary, routine day
subway, work, bars, fags, sleep, nothing.'

R. heard this said at a AA meeting. "Maybe I don't want to change. Maybe there are some people too damaged to change." He remembered Sandy, a drug-addled teen in Texas when he was in high school, lamenting this. She and her infant daughter and her lesbian lover against the world. She got busted for dealing and the police were threatening to bring her case to the D. A. unless she snitched on her supplier and her friends. Over a few ounces of marijuana, in her case. No wonder she drank.

R. could be at peace in the woods, no mirrors there. No superego, no pock-faced man at the levers calling the shots. No Procrustes bed to fit into, or off with your (natural born) feet. No "the fierce, complicated struggle of fighting males," as Jack London aptly phrased it.

What does appearance matter, your image, that you present to society?

On a social level, quite a lot. Competitive juices flow, there are limited slots for skilled workers and so on. Infighting, and the pecking order, place in the herd issues, quite a lot, but crack open the shell and there are other layers, biology, psychology, a cosmic mirror. How ya doing there?

R. flashed back to Iraq often, these days. Night-patrols, minefields. The specialist would cross a highway, go out in a field, and reconnect 100 yards down the road. They'd wait around for hours. A small puff, every so often. A larger puff, every so often.

"How was it?" R. asked the returning corporal.

"Hell on earth," was the reply.

A year later he was visiting him in a V.A. hospital. The right side of his face was gone.

Dude did a tour of duty in Iraq
Didn't think he was ever comin' back
Shells explodin' on the roadside,
Buddies loadin' body bags, nowhere to hide.
Crazy Capabarra
Crazy Capabarra.

R. would turn the radio up for certain songs.

'Talked to the man at the factory,
said 'son if it was up to me,'
worked for awhile in a refinery,
in the shadow of the penitentiary,

born in the USA,
born in the USA.

March called and there was rising excitement in his voice. "First, that complainant, I found her name and address. She lives in Oklahoma now. Second, Marjorie B--, your nurse, finally agreed to talk to me. She dropped a bombshell. Ready? Dr. Fairchild's got a drinking problem. It's fairly well known, she says. He keeps a flask of Jack Daniels in his scrubs. Drinks while he's making rounds, in between examining patients. She's witnessed it first hand, she says.

"She says he's joked about it with the nurses, once or twice. "High functioning," he says, tapping his pocket fondly.

"Jesus, son of God, isn't that illegal?" R. exclaimed vehemently.

"It is," affirmed March warmly. "Illegal, scandalous, and—highly illegal."

"What's the next step now?" R. practically screamed.

"I'll fly down and meet with complainant #1," replied March. "I've already made an appointment with her. I'm flying out tomorrow, on a jumbo. Later this week, you'll notice a debit in the retainer account. I'll be needing more soon."

"Whatever. Keep in mind I'm on a tight budget, will you?"

"I will," replied March. "We're making progress."

"Will Marjorie testify to that? Does she have tenure there, or whatever it's called?"

"We'll cross that bridge when we come to it. Have a nice evening," March said, and hung up.

March Nesmith's friendly, smiling face gleamed invitingly on his website 24 hours a day. Among his credentials he noted,

1. worked with the local FBI
2. worked with the watch commander of the local sheriff's department
3. worked with investigators working at the D.A.'s office
4. criminal defense attorneys.

March Nesmith took the most important call of the day, sitting in the Denver airport lounge, from his wife Maryanne.

"Hi March. Latest crisis, I want to ask Dad." March's two children, James and Lydia, were both teenagers, James a senior in high school, and Lydia in 9th grade.

"What now?" March joked. "Terrorist bomb threat in the cafeteria?"

"Almost," Maryanne replied gaily. "Lydia's school newspaper article is rocking a few boats here. It came out today, titled "Why I Am A Lesbian."

"Isn't she a little young to be making definitive announcements?" sighed March a bit wearily.

"Apparently not," Maryanne laughed. "She blames the slumber parties we have here."

"Honestly, Maryanne, the slumber parties. Tell me more."

"She says that when her friends come over for a slumber party, they have too much fun, hanging out, listening to music and talking about boys. And she prefers talking about boys than actually dating them."

"Oh really," March replied. "Slumber parties, huh?"

"Maybe we should be doing alittle surveillance," Maryanne teased.

March laughed, and looked around the lounge area. Two teenagers drinking coffee, avidly tuned to their IPads. An Asian male checking the Arrivals/Departures board. The walk of humanity to his right, or rather the slide, on a beltway.

"Oh, I dunno, I don't think at that age..." March began.

"It's so now for them though," replied Maryanne. "They feel things intensely."

"Only a phase," said March, hopefully.

"The school psychologist called, and strongly recommended we schedule a visit, her and Lydia. She wants to talk to her. Also, the school principal called. He'd like to talk to us."

"Oh great, just great," answered March. "Well I'm sitting here waiting for my connection. Maybe I could text her, tell her I love her and miss her, and remind her gently that actions have consequences. With an LOL."

"Why LOL, that's Laughing Out Loud? That would infer we're making fun of her."

"Oh, thought it signified Last On Line. I'm behind on the youth stuff Maryanne, help me out here. Instagram, webcams, darknets, I dunno."

Maryanne sighed. "The kids, it's a brave new world. With their gadgets."

"Speaking of surveillance, how goes your case, any further info on doctor sex ring stuff? Sounds exciting, if kind of tacky."

--"Well, she sounds out of it, to be honest, and this

happened so many years ago, like 30 year ago. Time'll tell I guess. I interview her tomorrow. My plane is running two hours late."

"Be safe dear," Maryanne sighed.

--The gentle tone in her voice reminded him why he married her.

March's hair was a little rumpled, but professional looking enough. He'd been grilled on the stand by many a judge and attorney. He was adept at testifying, and presenting the information he uncovered, if it came to that.

In this situation, providing a sympathetic ear, being a sympathetic listener, would be fundamental to progressing the case.

When March stepped off the plane in Oklahoma City, and rented a car, he rented a budget car. He booked a room in a budget motel, near the freeway.

Not a Motel 6 but not the Hyatt either, or the Marriott.

He liked this kid R. A 25 year old, a veteran. Foster kid. This car accident, a tough break. He'd testified in medical malpractice cases before. But he wasn't a doctor. Often, regrettably, it came down to who's attorney could outshine the other.

R.'s injuries might be heal-able, R. could be jumping the gun, given his paranoia, maybe from Post Traumatic Stress Syndrome. He advised him to have a series of photos taken immediately to preserve the "evidence" as it were. Also, to assemble "Before" and "After" head and face shots in a scrapbook, and update them every couple of weeks.

His job was to uncover prior wrong-doing by the

doctor. That would establish a modus operandi, an M.O., fundamental to building a case. "Brick by brick" the saying goes in evidence law.

His rented Taurus cruised through a windy autumn Oklahoma morning, into the ragged, ramshackle part of town. Garbage cans lined the street, not having been picked up in days, from the look of it. Dilapidated stairs led to tiny porches with tattered, torn screen doors, in dingy row houses. Two pit bulls barked at each other, each behind a chain link fence. The trees seemed to be prematurely nude, and beat, as if crying in sadness and distress.

"March Nesmith, private eye," March smiled, holding out his hand, and receiving a wan, forlorn stare. "Thank you for meeting me, you're probably very busy."

An ill-kept lady with a limp, in a faded housecoat ubiquitous with red roses, motioned him to an arm chair. She placed herself on a torn sofa, scratched herself in a few places, and turned on the tv.

"*I Love Lucy*'s on, I never miss it," she said robotically, like a zombie.

"Well, it'll be difficult to hear me over the tv," March said politely. "Perhaps I should come back another time."

"I like the pictures, I keep the remote on mute," giggled his interviewee. "Gotcha."

March laughed back, noting a gleam of humor behind her zombie mien.

"Peggy O'Doul, that's an Irish name?"

"I remember running along the beach, a little girl in a green bathing suit," she said suddenly, "I was carrying a colorful beachball, happy as a lark," she offered. "Oh so long ago."

"That's a beautiful memory," said March warmly. "Like I mentioned on the phone, I stumbled across your complaint about a Dr. Fairchild, my client is a car accident victim, Dr. Fairchild is his surgeon. Do you remember our discussion?"

"Dr. Fairchild, oh yes, " she replied. "It was long ago. I'll never forget. He was young. I was young. Dr. Portiss, an orthopedist, my back doctor, introduced us at a party. Dr. Portiss invited me."

"What kind of party?"

"Well, you know. I'm from the poor side of town. To have two impressive gentlemen like that interested in socializing with me, that was quite flattering. A doctor taking an interest in a girl from the wrong side of the tracks. I felt lucky at the moment, like maybe I was catching a break.

"Oh, look at Lucy, crazy and walking around in drag in front of Ricky's boss. Ha ha," she pointed to the tv.

"Bryon, Dr. Portiss, said he had a friend, a colleague he wanted me to meet. I was more than willing to party with a couple of doctors. They were good looking guys and seemed very nice. Seen Dr. Portiss due to a back injury. He did chiropractor stuff, rubbing and rotating. I trusted him at first. He helped my back."

"I understand," responded March. "Tell me about the party. From reading your complaint, something went wrong."

Peggy paused. She looked dead at the tv, but her eyes were far away.

"They behaved sleazy, assholes" she replied bitterly. "They wanted swinger sex, to have a threesome. I said 'No."

"They kept plying me with drinks. Like a fool, I kept accepting. You have to understand. I was a junkie, in an abusive relationship. My boyfriend would beat on me, and throw me down the stairs. My back's damaged permanently now.

"I didn't care how, I needed to get out. But I had my limits. I didn't want to be their rag doll, though they offered to pay. I remember they ganged up on me, and pulled off my clothes. Dr. Portiss held me from behind, and the other, Dr. Fairchild, put his penis in my mouth. I felt dizzy, and started to pass out. I hold my liquor well, I'm sure they slipped a pill into my drink.

"I could feel and experience what was happening, but I couldn't move. They were slapping me around, lewd and insulting. Every so often they'd be tender, and pet my hair. They jeered at me, and meanwhile Dr. Fairchild forced me. It went on for hours, I passed out. I woke up in Dr. Fairchild's bed the next morning.

"He came out from taking a shower, wrapped in a towel, and said he had to go to work. He gave me a hundred dollar bill, 'here's a Benjamin,' he said, 'take a cab, go home. Now."

"I had a hangover, and did what he said.

"I called him a day or so later. I wanted to tell him what a pig he was. He never returned my calls. Like he never knew me."

"The bloom of youth, ah rose of yesterday," Peggy said, perhaps a bit mockingly, and shocked March into present time, away from her mesmerizing narrative.

"I'm so sorry," he said, patting her hand spontaneously.

"There's two sides to every story ha ha," she replied enigmatically.

"There always is," agreed March heartily.

"Come see my cats," Peggy whispered, like a little girl. March gave her his hand, and they proceeded down the hall to Peggy's bedroom.

"There's Tangerine, and there's Patches. They are my babies," she cooed.

Tangerine and Patches gazed up curiously. Tangerine sat on a colorful madras comforter. Patches, after a moment's interest, gazed aloofly from a chair.

"Oh, it was so long ago, what does it matter? He called about two months later. He seemed genuinely upset that I was upset. He said he was sorry."

"Yes," said I, "I may be a prescription junkie, due to major back problems, but I've got values. Anyway, we worked out an agreement. He said he felt terrible and promised me $10,000 to help with my education, if and when I decided to go back to school." "Later I explained the situation to Dr. Portiss and we worked out a similar arrangement."

"May I use your bathroom?" inquired March suddenly.

"Down the hall to your left."

March did his business there, and sneaked a peek in the medicine cabinet. Numerous prescription medications in bottles resided there, including quaaludes, valium, amyl nitrate, and oxycontin, and percocet.

March returned, and together they sat on the back porch. Birds twittered in the trees.

"Did they get you hooked on drugs?" March asked. "You filed a complaint, remember, and alleged that in the body of the complaint."

"Oh, you know. How could I not say that? I came to Dr. Portiss with severe back problems. He put me on qualuudes and oxycontin. My lawyer at the time urged me to put it all out there, in red letters. Apparently a doctor having sex with a patient, even with consent, is a huge No No. Honestly, I was looking for more money out of them, and I got it, in return for settling out of court. And I got."

"Tell me," said March.

"They each gave me an additional $20,000. To be honest, their money helped me make a new start, I have to say ha ha. Tweedleum and Tweedledee. Out of their league messing with Peggy.

"You should talk to my girlfriend Suzanne. They ran around with her for awhile. She also was looking for a break."

"Last name," queried March.

"Suzanne Susie. Lost touch with her years ago. Living near Austin, Texas, last I recall."

"I will look her up," March said warmly.

Peggy walked March to the door. "It wasn't all bad," Peggy remarked wistfully. "I was married 20 years or so, and have two wonderful children. I straightened out my life, got off the painkillers for many years. Exercise, diet, rehab. After my divorce though, working at Walmarts, on my feet all day, my aching back. Shooting pains through my legs and buttocks constantly. A herniated disc, sciatica. I don't know what to do with my right leg at night."

March exited into a chilly autumn afternoon. He clopped down the rickety steps, and the two pitbulls across the way started barking furiously.

March wanted to strangle them, if looks could kill.

"What did I expect?," March wondered wearily. "Not much of a sex ring so far," he muttered in his rearview mirror, backing out of Peggy's driveway, twisting his neck awkwardly, narrowly averting a half-open garbage can, and turning towards his motel. "Got a second name anyway."

"Poor baby," Britney greeted Kimberly and threw her arms around her.

"It's rough," Kimberly affirmed. "Life is turning my presumptions into a fine dust..."

"Well, this could be worse," said Britney, on the bright side. "We could all be dead in a terrorist explosion tomorrow."

"It feels like monsters just below the surface, waiting to reach out and grab, if you stumble, or fall into a hole."

"God, it's awful," Britney agreed. "Bad things happen to good people.

How is he?"

"Well, I don't know. Seems to be coping, healing, says he needs his space. He's lucky to be alive."

"And your dad?"

"My dad's back home, seems fully recovered, after a very scary incident, thank God."

"It's a vale of soul-making," a poet said. "What doesn't kill us makes us stronger. Each day is a blessing."

"Easy to say. Until the monster grabs your ankle and pulls you into the pit again," replied Kimberly bitterly.

"Let's go for a walk, that's why we're here," encouraged Britney.

They began walking down a woodland path. Britney, with her tomboyish affinities, an avid hiker, arranged for this fresh air afternoon, and break back to nature, for Kimberly. She was hoping to cheer her friend up, help her refresh anyway.

The woodsy path, filled with elm trees, with broad leaves, the mighty oak, linden trees, poplar trees, the whitish ash, pine trees, provided a charming backing to their afternoon walk. The leaves were changing colors. Indian summer's last hurrah seemed to announce, like the loudest trumpet in the orchestra before the orchestra put down its instruments, and closed their cases.

"What does your Mom think? How is she handling this?"

"Mom's a trooper, you know. She's a nurse, so my dad's in good hands. She's a hardheaded woman, that's how she projects to me. But I know her, she's got a good heart. My dad and her are good role models, I'd be happy to have a marriage like hers basically. Though of course, we'd have better sex."

Britney laughed. "There you go," she encouraged.

"Seriously, each day is a blessing. My mom tells me not to expect too much from R. for awhile. She says when men say they need their space, be prepared. This may take awhile."

"Do your mother and father like R.?"

"Oddly enough, they do. He's kind of a dark horse, an underdog, a foster child and all, but very bright, and they understand that."

They arrived in a clearing with a couple of picnic tables. Birds sang all around them, in the canopies, from nearby branches. A mild breeze ruffled the treetops. A sunny afternoon.

"How's veterinary school?" asked Kimberly.

"Doing well. How's nursing school? Have you managed to catch up after missing a couple weeks."

"I suppose," said Kimberly. "Don't really want to talk about school. Busy enough, keeps me occupied. This other stuff, my heart, my aching heart."

"Well, it's lovely here!" Britney gushed. She opened her Evian water, and offered Kimberly a bottle. "Look around, the greenery, the colors, the birds. I'm working in a veterinary clinic, we have an owl there, an owl with a broken wing? It's the most darling thing."

"Will the wing mend? What will happen?"

"We don't know, time will tell. A farmer found it tangled in a barbed wire fence, poor thing. If it does heal, it will take months. Probably be released to a bird sanctuary, if it's able to fly. It's wilding days are probably over."

"Life and death, and death and life, it's all around us, we don't want to know," said Kimberly.

"Kimberly, didn't you mention R. likes birds?"

"Oh yeah, he's very attuned to birds. Feeds them every day, on his terrace. He's got his favorites. A hermit thrush is one."

"Let me look this up," said Britney, pulling a bird book from her pack.

"Yup, hermit thrush. I should learn about this." She read.

"Hermit thrushes breed in boreal and high elevation conifers and mixed woods, where it forages mostly on the ground, for invertebrates and berries. It winters in varied habitats, even shrubby, suburban thickets. Northern and eastern varieties have rusty wings and tails, lighter in the Midwest. Their song is a flute-like series of notes, Audubon described as a "sweet jumble", that turns the woods into a "cathedral."

"Does he have any other favorites?"

"Barn owls, if I recall."

Britney flipped the pages. "Yup, barn owls."

"Ooh, these are strange," Britney cooed shrilly. "Look at this Kimberly."

She pushed over the book and Kimberly looked at the picture. "Strange indeed," she cried. They both laughed. "That pure white, heart-shaped face, what a killer," Kimberly cried.

Britney read eagerly, "it preys on mice and other rodents. The species is strictly nocturnal but rarely observed in flight even at dusk. Its voice is a bone chilling, screeching hiss, often given in flight."

"Oooh," said Kimberly. "What about hoo hoo? You know, the wise owl."

"Many owl types," said Britney. "I don't know. Funky, feeds on numerous live mice each day. Well, the farmers loved them, that's for sure."

"What else you have there?" said Kimberly,

regarding her surroundings. She was ignorant about birds, though they flew by her every day. Never thought about them really.

They looked around, down the path, and up in the canopy. Many birds looked back, no doubt, but they were camouflaged. Every now and then, they could see one sitting on a low branch, or flying by. The air was sweet and clear, and they drank their water and Britney flipped through her book.

"Here's the red-tailed hawk. A raptor, like the owl. Enemy of assorted varmints, and also songbirds. They eat songbirds."

"The red-tailed hawk is the most widespread American raptor. There are seven subspecies, they range in plumage from whitish to dark brownish. The reddish tail and husky, full-winged shape are recognizable throughout red tail's range. They hunt mostly rodents from perches or soar, and dive on them from mid-air."

"Wonder if there are any in these woods?" said Kimberly uneasily.

"They hunt rodents, Kimberly," Britney laughed.

"Given all that's happened, I'm paranoid," responded Kimberly, nervously.

"Good to hear you laugh, Kimberly. It's all so interesting," Britney remarked, "worlds and worlds are rolling over."

"Yeah," said Kimberly. "We each end, but it never ends."

PART 2

3

Dr. Fairchild made an unpleasant discovery, his patient R. was asking questions.

"Uh oh," Dr. Fairchild exclaimed, to his bulldog Pugs, when he learned that there were inquiries made about his record, his practice, and in particular his drinking habits.

Dr. Fairchild was a distinguished surgeon on the record, with an office in the prestigious Marymount Medical center. Scores of hospitals invited him to perform surgery at their facilities.

He lived in an affluent neighborhood, in the tony section of Fairly, in a large house, fairly described as a mansion, with its stately colonial pillars, and Spanish Mediterranean split level design.

Dr. Fairchild had two sons. Jonathan, a strapping, handsome lad with wavy brown hair and blue eyes, after his freshman year at Stanford, boasted a 3.6 GPA, and played on their nationally ranked rugby team.

Nolan, his second son, class president at his prep school, finished his junior year with a 3.8 GPA, and scored over 750 on his SATS. He was already 6'2" tall, with blondish, wavy hair, and a winning smile.

Penny Fairchild, their mother, made a successful career in interior decoration and design. She built networks and connections with the high-end real estate agents in the area, over many years. New homes and young, affluent newlyweds were her specialty. She also played tennis and golf. She was on a number of committees, supporting local works, including the Connecticut Museum of the Arts, and the Hartford Ballet.

She was buxom, bubbly, and until recently content with the life she and her husband were living. It hadn't always been so.

They had met at a church picnic, when Arthur was in his residency. He was generally exhausted with the 16 hour days, and the hospital duties and rigors. Med school and his internship were grueling experiences enough. The learning curve was steeper than ever, in his surgical residency. He seemed wooden, and a bit pompous, and also a bit clinical, when they began dating. She had "a nose for a winner," her mother told her.

They had a way of coming together, for two alpha personalities with bright futures ahead of them.

Dr. Fairchild learned to lean on her in domestic matters, even before they were married.

She was so brisk, and efficient, she seemed a genie to him sometimes, so neat, and punctual and upbeat. Not to mention she grounded him.

He began to loosen up and trust her. They talked about marriage and having a family.

Life seemed to him like a fast moving train, and he met her in time, and she lifted him on board. Or maybe, helped him find his seat on board. His partying days were over. His ballroom days were over. So it progressed, and they built a life for themselves, two affluent professionals, with ambitions and goals that drove them to greet the day eagerly, and with great expectations.

Now in their mature years, they had hired a youthful servant Mitsy, an African American, from the New Haven slums.

"Higher taxes, always higher taxes," they complained. "Surgeons do such important work, you'd think they'd have an exemption or a deduction," Penny exclaimed consolingly. "Ivy League school for Nolan, and property taxes keep rising."

Their favorite book was *Atlas Shrugged,* they'd read this together in bed, on many occasions.

They were getting tired of the bonechilling winters. They were almost ready to retire to Hawaii, they joked.

So Dr. Fairchild said "uh oh," when Nurse B-- said pointedly one day out of the blue, "Jack Daniels should not be going into surgery with you, doctor."

Dr. Fairchild said "uh oh" when a well-respected orderly, Secret Hero, passed him in the hall and said, "No drinking on the job, right, Doctor?"

So, all was not as rosy as it appeared on the surface. Due mainly to his high pressure work environment, and the attendant stresses, performing complex surgery day in and day out, a couple drinks before dinner developed into a drink after breakfast, a drink after lunch, nips on the job, in addition to a couple drinks before dinner.

Did his drinking compromise his surgery?

The doctor thought it improved his results. His long

drinking history slowly built over time. "I'm immunized to alcohol," he'd tell himself. "I've built up a tolerance, and hold it well."

On the other hand, signs of aging were manifest. He was 51 years old. His golf game was off 5 or 7 strokes, at a mediocre 83 or 85. When he played tennis with Nolan on the weekends, he got run all over the court. He showed a little paunch and his wife was quick to tease. She remained shapely, for her age, having recently taken up biking.

He was deciding on easing into a retirement horizon, in the next couple of years.

These questions unsettled him. R. mentioned frankly he'd smelled alcohol on his breath, when being prepped for surgery, and the doctor, feigning shock, denied this. However, apparently R.'s concerns were getting around.

His brilliant career heretofar insulated him, and he manifested an arrogance about his faut paux. "It loosens me up for surgery in a good way," he'd argue righteously to himself. "It's a good thing."

The flask in his scrubs, "that's backup," he reasoned.

It's true he had a string of complaints filed against him. It was a litiginous society, all around him. Many were without merit. Anyway, he was human, he told himself. He made mistakes. "To err is human."

Meanwhile his wife had demons of her own. Age and boredom were playing catch up on her mind. One child in college, the other soon to be. She'd be an empty nester. She wanted special moments, wanted a shot at excitement, a thrill every so often. Going to Vegas with her girl friends once a year was not enough. Her condo in Florida was nice, but her husband rarely took the boat out.

She had an appointment with Drew Corliss, an attractive broker, to consult on a design for his living room. She wanted more, she wanted to bag him.

Dr. Fairchild hunched over a desk in his study, going over his checklist for tomorrow.

1. Dorothy Traynor. 1:30 p.m. Smaller nose. Higher cheeks. No jowls. Fairly common procedures.
2. Jane Charmion. 3:30. Major re-constructive surgery. Following a tragic incident with her pet monkey. The monkey, apparently distressed at a house guest, Ms. Charmion's friend, disturbing and intruding on their domestic tranquility, viciously attacked both women. The newspapers had run with it. Her friend died in the attack. Jane came in to hospital, with half her face ripped off. "Leave a lot of time for that one," he thought. "Make a little history."

Dr. Fairchild cast a glance at his schedule later in the week. He was also due to perform surgery on a young women whose face had been doused with hydrochloric acid. Jesus! A lurid week, indeed.

When Dr. Fairchild checked in next day, Secret Agent, the orderly, or whatever his name was, gave him a stony glance? Or did he?

He was getting paranoid.

A song from his high school days popped absurdly into his head, and he began whistling.

Paranoia strikes deep
into your life it will creep,
starts when you're always afraid
step out of line, man come and take you away.

Steady on," he admonished himself. "Lives are at stake."

Over the next few days, R. visited his friends for camaraderie and counsel.

First, Connor. Connor was a husky, broad-shouldered guy, with luxurious red hair, and a full red beard. R. did a stint with him at the pinball factory, and they had spent time together, listening to music, chugging beers after work, and doing the dating scene, a few double dates in his factory days, before meeting Kimberly. They had been friends in college.

Connor greeted him with a full body hug at the door. His girlfriend Colleen gave R. a peck and a hug. Colleen was a willowy young lady, with long hair, and pretty, big, round eyes.

"Where have you been?" Connor roared. "I've called and texted you 20 times."

Connor was renting a cottage, towards the back end of a housing development, under construction. The construction gig could last months. Connor's cottage was a perk, that came with the job.

"Would you like a cup of coffee or tea?" Colleen offered, while they settled down in the living room.

"What kind of tea?" R. inquired.

"Well, green tea, chamomile, Earl Gray, peach,

cranberry, oolong black tea, Constant Comment, orange spice."

"How about Constant Comment," R. replied. "About how I feel, here in the community. Who's Earl Gray anyway, is he from the House of Lords?"

"I don't know ha ha," Colleen smiled, and Connor chuckled.

"I remember your music, you've got talent," Connor recalled.

"I dunno," replied R. deprecatingly.

"The cover of *Rolling Stone* for this guy," Connor opined to Colleen. "You should write about your accident. You're looking alright dude. Remember this?" Connor gestured, raising his right arm.

"I remember. I visited you at the hospital." Connor was a motorcycle buff, he cracked up his bike a couple years ago, took a bad fall skidding on a wet freeway. "'More morphine, more morphine,' you'd call groggily."

"Don't remember. They put five titanium screws in my arm, fuse the broken bones together. I don't even feel it anymore."

"You're saying you're numb?" R. joked.

"My arm feels fine. No pain. Maybe a bit constricted in range. Maybe better than ever. I'm a bionic man now."

"Good for you," R. said warmly, sipping his Constant Comment. "Um good," R. said appreciatively.

"Well, with that cap on your head you look like Al Pacino in Serpico."

"I feel like Al Pacino in Scarface."

"That was Robert De Niro," Colleen reminded him gently.

"Oh, whoever," replied R.

Connor gave a long, appreciative whistle when R. took off his cap. "Your crazy ass got in some accident. You look like a Mohawk."

"I experienced brain swelling," said R. "They opened me up to relieve the pressure. They sewed me up and these sutures, well Frankensville, man. Now I know where that guy was coming from."

Colleen came around to take a closer look. She laced her hands gently on his shoulders. "You're healing," she said. "You're gonna recover. That's a great outcome."

"Just like a woman, to see the sunny side of things. Thanks, Colleen," R. exclaimed and turning, held her hand for a moment. "Are you jealous?" R. chided Connor.

"You're welcome," Colleen replied, squeezing his hand lightly, and withdrawing her hand. "You should be happy. Your hair's already starting to grow back. Soon the sutures will be removed, and any scarring will be totally covered over by your hair."

"But I'm on a roller coaster," R. confessed. "Serene one day, and angry the next," R. interrupted her, appealing to Connor. "I smelled alcohol on my surgeon's breath, when they brought me in that night. The guy seems off to me. I've hired a private detective. We've unfinished business."

"Dude, fuggedaboutit. Kimberly, man. Kimberly's gorgeous." Connor and Colleen met Kimberly at George's graduation party, and the hospital. Colleen and George were classmates, and friends.

"Kimberly's great. She nursed me back from the underworld for two months. Her parents took me in, and they treat me almost like their son. God knows where I'd be without Kimberly."

"That's the ticket," encouraged Connor. "You'll look back and laugh about this crazy ass accident one day. Home cooked meals. Alittle Tender Loving Care. Rest and Relaxation. Why didn't Kimberly come with you? We would have liked to see her."

"Like I said, I'm having problems. Kimberly's dad had a heart attack, or something. I feel guilty."

"Is he alright?" asked Colleen.

"Yes, he's back home. False alarm apparently. I got to figure out what I want to do with my life. Med school's out now. It's hard."

It's hard," Connor agreed. "I'm going to start my own business The House Doctors. Renovation and reconstruction. Got a good gig now, but want to be my own boss."

Connor threw his arm across R.'s shoulder, and walked him outside to his car. "Forward, march. Don't look back," he advised.

For awhile R. , Connor and Peter had been best buddies. Where Connor was husky and large, Peter was wiry and slender. Where Connor was blue-collar and valiant, the salt of the earth, Peter was artistic, lofty, and also a bit hyper, on occasion. They'd thrown the I-Ching the night before Peter left for the Peace Corps, and Africa. R. received "inner peace" (kind of ironic R. thought, given his circumstances now), Connor "warrior", and Peter "unrealized, with travel recommended."

Peter earned his spurs in Africa. He'd trekked to a remote location, and taught the villagers various things, reading , writing, and arithmetic, basically. He claimed to have learned "immensities."

On his return, Peter landed a job at a Film Arts foundation, and directed their endeavors, to create a credible platform for independent filmmakers in America.

Peter was also a romantic, and did well with the ladies. "I'm 25," he'd say, "I want to live before it's time to go."

R. and he were good friends, but also danced around each other to a degree. Peter's artistic views were varied, multilayered, and sophisticated. He'd graduated with a Bachelors degree in English, like R. His reading on his own was extensive, not only English literature, Fitzgerald, Hemingway, D. H. Lawrence, he dug them all. Also adored the French expressionists like Van Gogh, Gauguin, Monet, Manet, Renoir, and Degas. Admired surrealist poets like Rimbaud, Verlaine, Baudelaire, to name a few.

"Don't tell me I look like Al Pacino in Serpico," R. joked, after a hug, "I'm gonna scream."

"Alright," Peter promised. "You look like Al Pacino in *Dog Day Afternoon*, happy now?" Peter joked back.

"What a multitudinous, refreshing, variable cat you are," R. exclaimed. "How do you like your job?"

Peter shrugged. "It's okay. Worried about you, if you want to know. Connor called and filled me in."

"I'm 25 and I don't know what to do," R. exclaimed. "I got into med school but after this, I'm getting a message loud and clear, it's not in the cards."

"Med school's a long haul," agreed Peter sympathetically. "You're a born writer if you ask me.

This is grist for the mill."

"You mean my accident?"

"Your accident. What doesn't kill you makes you stronger, indeed," Peter encouraged.

R. pulled off his cap.

"Ouch," Peter exclaimed dramatically. "Somewhere something is torn."

"What?" R. replied.

"A bard said that, I think Verlaine. Sobbing fountains, anyway."

"Have a drink of water?" Peter offered him bottled water.

R. took a few slow sips. They were sitting in a café, down the block from Peter's new office. When R. took off his cap, he heard a buzz, and hushed tones, but perhaps this was his imagination.

"Here you have a girlfriend, good for you."

"Yeah, she's super. I don't deserve her," confessed R. miserably.

"You deserve her, you deserve her. You're a gifted guy. Don't forget."

"I feel maimed. I hate my surgeon, I smelled alcohol on his breath, the night they wheeled me in to the hospital."

"These rich doctors," Peter agreed readily. "So enabled, by a system where patients are little more than coded numbers, an endless stream of them. They can be insensitive as hell. My mother died on the table, pancreatic cancer. Her doctor seemed robotic when he told us she'd died. No emotion. Maybe they're trained to behave like that."

"What should I do, Peter?" R. implored, embarrassed.

"You're an artist. Feel your way. God will tell you. Or if not God, the heavens."

"Didn't you tell me once you were an atheist?"

"No atheists in the foxhole," Peter quipped. "Africa changed me. You're not the only one with problems. I'll have bouts of malaria, fevers, the shakes, for the rest of my life, probably. Relax. Breathe deep. You'll receive a sign," Peter said in confidential tones, confidently.

Indiana Jones, with his too large hands and feet, and tall, lean physique, reminded R. of an Indian guide, in colonial days. Maybe because Indiana led R. on many a hike in their college years, up and round Connecticut mountain ranges including the Berkshires and the Appalachian range.

However, Indiana was not Native American, though his high cheekbones, angular jaw, and long brown hair, parted in the middle, and cascading down his back, in a pony tail, seemed to announce otherwise.

"In another life," R. would joke with him, following behind him, on a trail in the middle of nowhere, surrounded by thick scrub brush. "Its a little farther, right over here," Indiana would call encouragingly. Half an hour later, they were still meandering through dodgy trails amid the thickets.

"A little farther Jones," R. began calling him.

When R. drove over one Sunday afternoon, he remembered their frequent, sometimes laughable adventures together hiking. There was the time Indiana, Connor and he came to a rapidly flowing stream they needed to cross. R., fearful he would be knocked over, began parsing the advantages to staying behind, with his notebook, and meeting them later on the way. Besides, they noted that there were a few steep ledges coming up, and R. was wearing shorts, while the others wore sturdy dungarees.

"I'll stay here, with my notebook, and meet you on your way back," R. decided.

They leaped into the stream, like two yahoos, and while buffeted and swayed, made it across, no problem, then disappeared down a ridge. R. found plenty to enjoy just where he was. When he got restless, he went for a hike of his own, and doubled back to the side of the stream. No sign of them. Darkness fell. The breeze stiffened, and the temperature dropped. Round about 9 p.m., there they came, looking exhausted. "Where were you?" R. cried. "We said around 7 o'clock."

"We found this great beach. So beautiful. The tide came in so suddenly. We were backed up against a cliff, and barely made it out of there. Connor lost his shoes, swept out by the tide."

Connor was in his bare feet. The rocks and dirt and sand were not easy on bare feet. Connor walked for eight miles, chomping up his feet pretty badly, wincing in pain, and by the end of the trek, hobbling. He would not take a shoe from R., wouldn't hear of it. Indiana said, "serves him right, he knows he should have checked carefully, and not left his shoes on the beach."

They laughed about that for a year or two.

Indiana greeted R. warmly, with an elaborate handshake that R. barely recalled from their trail days.

"Called you many times in the last week, and texted

also. Where were you?"

"Incommunicado," I guess, replied R. "It's been awhile. How's life in your neck of the woods?"

Indiana displayed his lean, muscled arms, and legs. "Keeping busy." Inside their house, R. renewed his acquaintance with Indiana's girlfriend Sarah, and their little baby Rose. Sarah was a slender young lady with long, sandy blonde hair, and tan face and arms. "She looks like Mother Nature's daughter," murmured R. Their baby Amanda, toddled around in diapers and t-shirt, with an oversized U. Conn hat on her head, she looked adorable. She came up to R. and looked up at him with big goo goo eyes. "Say hi, Amanda," Sarah urged. Amanda obliged with a sudden "hi," then teetered off to play.

"You're hooked up with the university now, Connor mentioned," R. said.

"How's that working out for you?"

"Love it, well enough," Indiana replied. "Learning about water treatment, on the job, to a degree, though I got my degree in environmental sciences. A classroom's one thing, real life's another."

"I hear that," said R. "I'm a little jealous. Being at loose ends you know."

"Did you know that tap water is generally safer than bottled water?" Indiana plowed on. "The federal EPA and state Department of Public Health enforce strict water quality standards for public drinking. On the other hand, the same standards do not apply to bottled water. And the Food and Drug Administration standards are not as stringent, and they only get involved in interstate commerce."

"Water, water everywhere, hopefully not poison," R. joked.

"Hopefully," Amanda chimed.

"Also, plastic bottles are made from PET, which is made from petroleum. Also, the production costs for a bottle, wastes about 3 to 4 bottles of water," Indiana pressed home his point.

"Whoa, who knew?" R. responded. They all sipped their tap water.

"Connor tells me you received admission to medical school, big congrats," Indiana said.

"I'm not going," R. replied. "I've decided." He pulled off his cap.

"You've been in an accident, " Indiana said. "How you're feeling is the main thing, the wounds will heal."

"I hate my surgeon, the guy had alcohol on his breath when they wheeled me in. To be honest, I keep suspecting he treated my head with reckless disregard."

"Dude, paranoia. Natural, I guess. You need to get outside yourself, relax, takes walks, enjoy nature, like we used to do. You ought to try Events and Adventures, that's where I met Sarah. They host 10-12 local events each month."

"Something for most every taste, horseback riding, wine-tasting, rafting, even jumping out of a plane," Sarah added.

"Step up your web presence. Facebook, Instagram. Get into the mix," Indiana urged.

"Facebook, with this face?" R. laughed.

"Wear your cap for now, do a selfie, folks love the look these days. It'll heal. Keep a positive attitude."

"Remember how we hiked in the Berkshires. Many a trail, obstructed by many a thicket, and underbrush, I thought we were lost."

"We never were," replied Indiana warmly. "Remember. We worked our way out of it, one way or another. Around, about, or through, we persevered. I'd find a way. Or you'd find a way. We were a sounder of thickets, but never trapped."

"Yes," said R. "I remember."

4

"Dr. Fairchild's office sent over the ER photos, the x-rays, and the CAT Scans. I've looked through your file. You are recovering well," he said firmly. Dr. Kranaidas was stocky and broad shouldered, with a sharp jaw and prominent chin, olive complexion, and abundant wavy salt-and-pepper hair.

His fingers lightly and expertly flew over R.'s face and head, lightly tapping here and there, but unlike Dr. Fairchild, not tugging or pulling. "The redness around your left eye socket is resolving nicely," he added.

"There's numbness in my lower lip, on the left side," R. noted.

"Hmm. You are lucky, young man. The nerve's stretched out, but not cut. Also, the muscle was beaten up but not cut. You should recover fully in a year to 18 months. Your lip will follow your smile, eventually. Good news for you."

His voice was calm and reassuring. R. liked him immediately.

"I have a problem with Dr. Fairchild, I smelled alcohol on his breath when they wheeled me into the ER. Also, he called me a 'deadhead,' in his office, during an exam the other day."

"Hmm," said Dr. Kranaidas again. "Perhaps a misunderstanding," he suggested.

"Do you doctors always have to stick together?" R. blurted impulsively. "I feel like I'm up against a wall here. But I like you, I'm glad I came here for a second opinion."

Dr. Kranaidas sighed. "You seem like a nice young man. You've been traumatized, you have to remember. Experiences can be distorted, under extreme conditions."

"No," R. replied. "He called me a 'deadhead.'"

"Tell me," Dr. Kranaidas offered gently.

"He was examining me, much like you are now, going over my wounds," R. explained. "He stood behind me so, and said 'deadhead.'"

Dr. Kranaidas signed again. "It's not easy doing surgery day in and day out. Each day we're in there, like a boxer in a ring. Our opponent, death, does not seem to tire. It keeps on coming."

"Well, doctors shouldn't be Death the Destroyer, and that's how he comes across to me. Like a flaming asshole. Like bad news," R. said vehemently.

"When I called him on it he said, 'oh, I heard you were a musician, and assumed the Grateful Dead were on your playlist, my son plays guitar, isn't that the moniker for Grateful Dead fans?'"

"That explains it then," said Dr. Kranaidas. "Perhaps he could have been more sensitive."

"When I expressed my displeasure at his poor choice of word and comment, given my traumatized condition and the injuries I sustained, he said, 'You're being hypersensitive.'"

Dr. Kranaidas sighed and said, "it's hard."

"Are you Greek?" inquired R. suddenly, shifting gears.

"I am," Dr. Kraniadas affirmed warmly. "How did you know?"

"I dunno," R. said shyly. "I visited Greece a couple of years ago. I love it there. Mousakka, dolmathakia, tiropytes. Umm…"

"My wife could give you a few recipes. I'm more of a meat-and-potatoes guy," he laughed. "Haven't been there in years."

"The Parthenon, the Acropolis, the cradle of western civilization. Socrates, Plato, Aristotle. The first western democracy. Aescylus, Euripedes, tragedy and comedy."

"They are more concerned about whether they should remain in the European Union these days," Dr. Kranaidas responded. "Things change."

"I wish I could wear Perseus' helmet, be invisible," R. confessed suddenly. Tears came to his eyes.

"It's hard," Dr. Kranaidas agreed. "We have to carry the weight, a bit like Sisyphus. You're young, you're what—25? Your whole life is in front of you," he encouraged. "By the way, if you feel harried or harassed, make a complaint to the hospital and the State Board of Health. Good luck," Dr. Kranaidas said, and shook R.'s. hand heartily. "Please do me a favor, hand this to the nurse on your way out."

"The end of the tunnel is not an illusion. There's a light at the end of the tunnel."

"Richard, that's beautiful. Tell me more," said Kimberly.

"I miss you. I need you. I woke up from a dream, with the words on my lips."

"I miss you, babe."

"How's nursing school? Wanna meet me at a motel tonight?"

"Have a quiz tomorrow. Ugh! My professor reminds me of the military, Ms. Ice Buckets, I call her. She served overseas, she says. How did you deal with it?"

"I dunno. They helped straighten me out, in a way. 'The early bird gets the worm. Get to the day before it gets to you,' kinda thing. In a foster home, abandonment is par for the course. It's an endless stream of desertion. Desert. Dessert. Wasteland. In the military, they won't let you alone but they won't abandon you either," R. replied. "It was an improvement."

"How are you feeling? What are you doing?"

"Take walks, sleep a lot. Avoid the mirror," R. replied. "Got good news from a doctor today, a second opinion. Tomorrow, I have an appointment with March, the private eye."

"Forward, march" said Kimberly playfully. "I'm so proud of you."

"R. , welcome to the jungle," March joked, waving him in expansively, motioning him to a well-appointed chair. March sat at an impressive oak desk, diplomas, certificates, and licenses, arrayed on the wall behind him.

"Coffee, tea, juice, water?"

"Water would be fine," R. responded.

"Portia could you rustle up a couple bottled waters for R. and myself," March slightly yelled through the open door. A brisk, perky blonde, in a pageboy style, bustled in with two bottles. "R., good to see you," she gushed, placing the Arrowheads within arm's reach, for R. and her boss. "One of these days you'll tell me your full name," she chided. She lay down a couple of Nashville napkins for R., and her boss. "So mysterious," she exclaimed, and hurried off.

"Did you know that tap water on the whole is healthier than bottled water?" said R., a touch mischievously. "I received a lecture on it the other day. The bottles are petroleum-based, according to my friend, an authority on the subject, or so he represents."

March offered up a toast. "To your friend. May we learn something new every day. But they're still legal right?" joked March.

"Yes," R. said.

"How about the Patriots this year?" March remarked, opening a thick file on his desk.

R. coughed nervously. March was mysterious about the reason for the meeting, other than to say it would be important. "Every so often I'll tune in if Tom Brady's playing. Baseball's my favorite sport though," R. countered.

"Too slow for me," said March.

"I'm old school, I like it slow I guess," said R.

"Old time baseball, yeah," March replied. "Those old timers were golden, giants of the earth. What's your favorite team?"

"The St. Louis Cardinals," offered R. "They named the team after a bird, more power to them."

"I grew up in Dayton, Ohio," March replied.

"I grew up near St. Louis, after moving up from Texas, first grade. Stan "The Man" Musial. A .331 lifetime batting average. 475 homers, 725 doubles. Led the Cardinals to three World Series championships during his career. Played on an All Star team a record 24 times. They said his peek-a-boo stance was like a kid looking around the corner to see if the cops were coming. Would have easily surpassed 500 home runs and 2,000 RBIs but spent a year in the Navy during World War 2. What a guy."

"Stan the Man Indeed," said March warmly. "Remember Stan, even though a wee tot at the time. Most Valuable Player three times or was it four?" March hesitated.

"Three or four, one of the greats," R. enthused. "One of the greats."

"Did you know ironically, they won a world championship again, the year after he retired," March asserted. "Lou Brock, a future Hall-of-Famer came on board that year."

"Didn't know that," R. replied.

"By the way, I won't charge you until we get on topic, no worries," March said, tapping the large folder on his desk.

"Hit me with your best shot," R. replied.

"You're a bright young man," said March. "How are you feeling? How's your recovery coming along?"

R. liked March, but there was no use pretending, he wanted to be honest.

"Depends on the day," R. replied. "Ups and downs you know, to be honest.

"Take long walks, sleep a lot, try to heal. I'm spending emotional energy on this Dr. Fairchild situation, hopefully you understand," R. began haltingly.

"The alcohol on his breath, first red flag," continued March. "Calling you 'deadhead' during an office visit, while examining your head wounds, a second red flag. Given your traumatized state, and serious wounds, I get it," replied March warmly. "You know what they say, a paranoid person sometimes has reason to be paranoid. Hey, I look over my shoulder when I walk out of here, to the parking lot in the evening. In your case, you may be picking up on a major issue. On the other hand…" March trailed off.

"Did you find anything?" R. questioned, cut to the chase.

"Let me tell you," March explained, tapping the file. "Dr. Fairchild is hooked up with several important Federal Board of Health commissions. Dr. Fairchild's received the Yale University medal for Excellence in Surgery. Dr. Fairchild was called in to consult on presidential surgery, with a recent president. Flew to Washington, D.C. and was among a team that operated on the president. He's close to being a superstar surgeon, if there is such a thing."

"The guy's got connections," R. responded.

"He's earned the respect of his colleagues, over many years," March corrected gently.

There was a pause. A pregnant pause.

"On the other hand," March continued. "Like I mentioned, there have been numerous complaints to the Connecticut State Board of Health. And then the trail goes cold," March continued.

"What do you mean?" R. queried.

"I did not find evidence of law suits," March said firmly. "Not one."

"Tell me," R. encouraged.

"On the other hand, also meeting Peggy O'Malley face to face. Peggy provided a second name. I found her. She will not talk to me, says nondisclosure is part of her legal agreement."

"Meaning?" said R. impatiently. "Please explain."

"He pays them off. Pays them well. To state a cliché, makes them an offer they cannot refuse," replied March. "We'll probably never know the terms of their agreement, or what he did."

"Hush money?" queried R.

"Hardly," March replied. "That's business as usual given his high profile position. He makes the big bucks because he's highly skilled, and what he does, there are serious risks involved always. I wanted to meet you here in my office to impress upon you how important you are. My first duty is to you, my client. For example, I will never divulge your identity to any party, without your permission, if we decide that the process moves forward. Having met Kimberly also, and spent alittle time with you both, I confess I have friendly feelings towards both of you. You're the kind of young people our country needs more of, bright, well-intentioned, with high ideals. I'd love to be able to read a headline like 'Private Eye Saves President From Serial Killer Sex Ring Surgeon.' Or 'Private Eye Uncovers Surgeon Sex Ring With Underage Girls.' Ah," March paused, alittle smile playing on his lips.

"Unfortunately, a little smoke maybe, but apparently no fire. And I do not want you to get your hopes up. Or run your bill up unnecessarily, on wild speculation, and improbable theories," March said.

"Alright," said R. "Yes. I get that. I received a second opinion from another surgeon, earlier this week, and he looked at the X-rays, the CT scan, the pictures, and the file, and concluded that Dr. Fairchild did a competent job," R. explained. "The muscles and nerves in my face are stretched here and there but not torn, and there should be no permanent nerve damage."

"Good news," March said warmly. "Happy to hear this, things are looking up."

"I still have a funny feeling about the guy. Almost like I've met him before," insisted R.

"Well, look, here's a thought. You could put your shoulder to the wheel, do a little research yourself, hunt around on the internet, there's a website or two that may help, I'll give you their names later if you want, see what comes up, if anything. If the second gal wants to speak with me…I'll consult with you, before paying her a visit."

"Sounds like a plan," said R. "I should probably be relieved."

"Yes, if I was walking in your shoes, I'd be relieved," said March. March walked him out to the parking lot, and patted him on the back. R. noted he looked over his shoulder, during the short walk, as if on cue.

"A man's gotta do what a man's gotta do," he explained. "Better safe than sorry," he jested, and smiled.

"You've received scores of complaints from your

patients over the years, but you continue in your arrogant ways, apparently. I'm more informed about it than you think. I know about your sex ring during your residency years in Texas. How you lured underage girls with promises of drugs and cash, and spiked their drinks and forced yourself on them, you and your cohort the orthopedist. You're also an alcoholic. You drink on your rounds, maybe even before surgery. You operate on your patients, on their brains, their hearts, with a surgeon's instruments, with saw, pliers and scalpels, while you're drunk."

"That's a heinous lie," Dr. Fairchild replied.

R. pulled a gun from his pocket, a snub-nosed .45. "What will it take for you to learn to respect your patients, doctor?"

R. began waving the gun wildly in the air.

Dr. Fairchild measured the distance to the door, but decided not to risk that, with R. blocking the way. His Iphone was out of reach. He stood behind his chair, against the wall, looking frantically for an angle, a way out.

Dr. Fairchild spoke calmly, seeking to lull R. with his dulcet tones. These were tones he employed to good effect to calm his patients before surgery, or giving lectures to the broader community at large. His voice dripped honey, and good reason.

"Young man," he began. "Put the gun away. Would you want to ruin your life and mine, in a moment's picque and distress? Commit an act under duress that you'll never forgive yourself for later? And for which society will never forgive you? We can talk about the issues. I'm a human being, I make mistakes. Big men don't need guns to settle their disputes and perceived grievances, that's not the way..."

"I'm not a big man," R. retorted. "I'm the incredible shrinking man you made me into. I'm miniscule because of you, God loves me anyway."

"You're breaking my heart," Dr. Fairchild replied.

"You already broke mine," R. cried and pulled the hammer back, and pulled the trigger.

In the moment R. pulled the trigger, letting loose a series of bangs, like firecrackers, Dr. Fairchild spun sideways, and fell to the floor screaming, "I'm hit, I'm hit. Help, help."

"How does it feel doctor?" R. stood over him, with blazing eyes.

The doctor began frantically feeling for his wounds. He felt dizzy, his adrenalin was pumping, and he felt like fainting, and perhaps he was a little intoxicated from a couple of nips from the flask earlier before their meeting.

Strangely, he could not find any bullet holes, when he pulled up his shirt and pants leg, and searched over his torso area. His clothes were disheveled, he was sweating profusely, but there was no blood.

"I fired blanks," said R. quietly, turned on his heel, and exited the room.

"By the way," R. declared, sticking his head back into the room, swinging the door wide. "I've filed a complaint with the hospital and the Connecticut State Board of Health, that I smelled alcohol on your breath, the night I was wheeled into the hospital, Jack Daniels, if I'm not mistaken, I've drunk enough to have a memory, and be able to ID this, and you performed surgery. Nurse B-- filed a complaint also. She will testify that she has observed you drinking alcohol on the premises a few different times, and she feels a responsibility under state law, to alert the authorities.

"I'm a sounder of thickets, around, over or through, doesn't matter to me," R. concluded and gently closed the door.

5

"Well, that's the mentality, what you're messin' with," Kimberly reproached him, almost coming to tears. "I don't want you to go to jail," she pleaded. "Did you think about that? How I would feel? How devastated I would be? Huh?"

R. back pedaled, with grim humor. "I dunno," he admitted. "Time will tell, it always does."

"It's all politics now, a political football. Within the D.A.'s office. Happy now?"

"Kimberly…Kimberly…don't desert me. It would kill me, please," R. pleaded. "You know how crazy that would make me."

Sade's song filled the room.

Your love is king,
your love is king.

"Me and you," she asserted, with tears in her eyes.

They quietly sipped their wine.

"Have not been living under a rock," R. replied, a bit haughtily. "Pick up any newspaper, cannot help but note the rash of police shootings, that are causing huge protests in Chicago, Washington D.C., and elsewhere. African Americans gunned down in highly suspect circumstances. I studied the clips of the Eric Garner take-down. Horrible travesty of justice. Big, overweight guy standing on a street corner. Rushed by two police officers, though he put up absolutely no resistance. Gang tackled, manhandled. Sat on, beat on, put in a strangle hold. Later died in a police van. A diabetic condition may have contributed, that he informed them about over and over. Murdered in broad daylight by two police officers. I read the papers. I get the drift," R. replied.

"That's me. Smooth operator," R., boasted.

Kimberly drank a sip of wine, and regarded him fondly. "NOT," she responded, in good humor. "They're considering arresting you. You have to play it cool. Be very careful. Fortunately, our testimonials for you are being taken into consideration. Also, fortunately for you, Dr. Fairchild is not inclined to press charges."

"Of course not. If he does his alcoholism issue will come out. That will be front and center in any discussion of the case. That would only be fair."

"Fair! What do you know?," Kimberly replied. "You're not a lawyer. You don't know how this will all play out. What's fair? When did that amount to much when dealing with the police? Have you been living under a rock for the last 20 years? Also, I shared my positive view, regarding your future, your sanity, and your mental health. They talked to Nurse B-- also, who informed them over the phone about the complaint you filed with the State Board of Health. She gave her support to you 100%."

"Let the chips fall where they may," R. bluffed. "I'm not afraid. I'm not going to be intimidated by an alcoholic surgeon."

"Richard, you can't go around drawing and shooting guns in a doctor's office, that's taboo."

R. sang Kimberly the Sade song.

You're giving me the sweetest taboo,
you're giving me the sweetest taboo.

"I have the Sade CD. I'm going to get it and put it on," R. said. No sooner said than done, he sprang up, and the room filled with sounds of Sade.

Western night, lover boy,
move through space with minimal waste,
maximum joy. No need to ask
he's a smooth operator, smooth operator…

She strode in black slacks and black sweater, and running shoes, rather like a tall black cat, to the center of the room, and they began dancing.

R. prepared a candlelight dinner for two. He imagined hushed conversation, quiet, romantic.

Instead it turned into a strategy session with regard to Dr. Fairchild.

"I've been waiting to tell you. Don't be upset. The D.A.'s office called. They spoke with my father, my mother, and myself. They are very concerned. They were considering arresting you," Kimberly divulged over desert.

"Why?" R. wondered.

"You made quite a spectacle over there," Kimberly replied.

"Theater. Of the absurd," R. replied. "All theater."

"Lucky for you my parents spoke up for you, and shared their positive impression about you."

R.'s days of playing the victim were numbered. He felt a bit more on top of the situation.

When he had returned home, he began preparing dinner. But first he had flipped on the player to his favorite classic and progressive rock station. Music blared loudly.

Runaway train on a one way track,
runaway train never looking back.

He cooked the grape leaves in a sizzling fry. He wrapped up the souvlaki into cute little portions. He boiled water and chopped up the mutton stew into bite size bits. After done cooking, he put them on skewers. It smelled delicious. He bought the cheese balls whole, in a package, all he had to do was warm them in the microwave once Kimberly arrived.

When Kimberly arrived, he showed her into his newly cleaned apartment, and she exclaimed "smells delicious." He saved a quality bottle of wine for transport to the table, in a large folded napkin.

"Kimberly, please call me," he had voice messaged her from his cell phone. "I'll cook dinner, mousakka, souvlaki, cheese balls, grape leaves, ??????."

R. hurried to a local market that carried the ingredients he needed.

All his instincts and intuitions told him there would be "back draft" from the crazy incident the day before in Dr. Fairchild's office.

However, he'd mailed the complaint to the State Board of Health, including Nurse B.'s-- complaint, that supported his own, and verified that Dr. Fairchild habitually drank alcohol on the hospital premises. He felt confident that such testimony would provide ample defense, and protect and defend him, if push came to shove. He felt liberated by having acted out. His days of being, and feeling a victim were receding in the rear view mirror, he fervently hoped.

The next day, R. pulled into a Jiffy Lube down the block from the library. A burly, bearded mechanic, with shoulder-length hair and tattoos visible on his muscular arms, in his short sleeved blue Jiffy Lube uniform, came up and said "what?"

"He doesn't care," thinks R.

"Oil change," said R.

"Pull it over here," the fellow snarled.

R. pulled his car up to the recently vacated "pit-stop." Fred, so his name tag said, got behind the wheel, and repositioned the car so he could drain the oil out, into the pan below.

"How long?" said R.

"About 25 minutes," said Fred. Fred didn't look up, and barely looked around, intent on his drudge task. R. could see "the boss" sitting in a little office off to the side, a baldish, blond guy with big muscles, head tilted to a computer screen.

"9 to 5 drones, so unhappy," R. thought. R. was suddenly glad to be alive.

"They too will soon be free," he thought. The boss doesn't care either, he concluded.

Earlier, R. had been cruising down the street, in the commercial district, and nearly gotten into an accident. It got him into his "who cares?" mode. Right in front of him, twenty yards ahead, a guy parked his car, and flung wide his door, overhanging the lane, into the oncoming traffic. A crusty, older guy with "duck's ass" hair gone gray, did not care, rummaging his backseat seemingly oblivious to the honking horns and several near misses, including R., who was forced to swerve into the second lane, barely escaping a collision, and pile up. Likewise the cars that followed R., swerving and dodging, at high speeds, two lanes suddenly turned into one. "F--ing car door open, on a busy street, sure why not?" R. clucked in his rear view mirror, at the ensuing chaos. A Dylan song played on the radio.

People are crazy, times are strange,
I'm locked up tight, I'm outta range,
I used to care, things have changed.

"Why do we have to be so servile, obsequious, subservient, fawning, to our 'bosses' in society? Why so abasing, prostrating, ingratiating, apple-polishing? Are we only time-servers, hirelings, a tool for the enterprise?

"Why cringe, bow, stoop, bend our knees? Why crawl, crouch, cower, kiss the hem of the boss' garment, throw oneself at their feet? Do I want to be an unctuous, oily, slavish, mealy-mouthed serving boy all my adult years? Do I need to be sycophantic, skulking, sniveling, and oh so abject and pliant the best years of my life?

"I want an employment where I am independent, my own man. I want an employment where I express myself. I want to work together, cooperate, guide."

"Be a teacher," replied Kimberly brightly.

"A teacher, that's a lot of work," said R.

Kimberly laughed. "How now brown cow," she jibed.

"No, that's not what I mean," R. sallied back. "Or maybe it is," he giggled.

"Only that it is so much responsibility, so time consuming, so societally engaged, so harnessed, as it were. A classroom full of kids. Me their teacher, really?"

"I think you'd make a great teacher," Kimberly encouraged enthusiastically. "You're an artist. You've got the learning, the skills. Your literary scope and breadth. You'd have to go back to school and take a few Education courses, do student teaching. You could do the coursework with your eyes closed, I'm sure," Kimberly reassured him, emboldened him.

R. was feeling empty, depleted, exhausted after knife-fighting death, and in a figurative way, with authority figures, super ego, all that.

He felt rather like a sheep in a paddock, penned, hedged, fenced in, corralled the past month. The car accident of course was the huge delimiter. He didn't like feeling enclosed, confined, surrounded, stockaded. Perhaps it was natural to fight rude circumstance with emotion, and personify the struggle. Perhaps R. projected a bit onto the doctor.

"Will you help me?" R. replied. "I talk big, but I don't

know, " R. trailed off. "I have to deal with bad headaches. My past..."

"I'll help you," Kimberly promised, with big, round eyes. "We'll be the dynamic duo, I'll be a nurse, you be a teacher."

"If only it were possible..." R. wondered, half-elated, half-depleted by the prospect, the difficulty of it all. "Doesn't the Administration present problems? You know, one hears or reads stories about school principals and their heavy hand and such. The Board..." R. equivocated, and wondered. "Who knows if there is a university around here offering education courses?"

"A teacher's college," Kimberly clarified. "They're around. UConn's got a reputable program, it's a half hour commute. It would be easy for you. They're over a few hills, you would need snow tires in the winter, with chains. As for Admin., there's always going to be supervisors where kids are involved. But think about it. Remember your school experience. Teachers have autonomy. Teachers rule the classroom. You'd make a great teacher, I'm sure of it," cried Kimberly excitedly.

"A classroom full of students, boys and girls, young men and young ladies, princes and princesses. His to mold, his to guide," thought R.

A one day substitute teacher gig maybe. He would take it slow and easy, feel his way along, observe, make mental notes, catch the drift of the enterprise, get his "school boy" on, make sure he was not allergic to the air, and the "airs" he would have to put on, being the room's resident authority figure.

He almost laughed out loud, imagining driving to

his first assignment. "Me an authority figure. Apolcalypse now," he joked with Kimberly.

Who was he? What was he doing? Why was he here on earth? Maybe this would help him find out. Or provide an interlude anyway, a possibility of finding out.

"Music and tears," a bard said, "I can scarcely tell the difference."

"Love and work," said Jung, "the two fundamental human endeavors." Well maybe he experienced enough music for awhile. His soil was wet with music.

The next day, R. picked up a text from Secret Hero, and called him back.

"Dude," said Secret Hero, "I've been texting you all week. What's happenin' with you (jhoo)? Come on over to the studio. We'll get down, you know. Freebase heart and soul, with the colors of our mind. Ha ha ha! We'll generate our energies into the sun, into the production of gnarly sonic space, sonic tapestries, we'll get twisted and entwined, we'll sell our dramas to ourselves, with modern technology, we'll create knock-out sonic landscapes that will dazzle the throngs, the millions, the masses," Secret Hero egged him on. "The first session's on me."

"Do you know anyone making money from music?" R. responded caustically, with a mocking tone. "Don't hustle da hustler…"

"It's not about money, man. I thought you were an artist. You know that. The millions got the gear now, it's out of the hands of the elite," Secret Hero replied confidently, "you know that be true. It's in our hands. It's about self-expression, self-realization."

"Self expression and self realization are fine," R.

responded cautiously. "But I have to pay the rent each month. I have to find a working gig and pronto. Do not want to be yanking on Kimberly's skirt hems, I already owe her $5,000 for splurging, and funding the private detective. I intend to pay her back before the year ends, or a good portion of it anyway."

"Oh yeah, I dig that. Neither a borrower or a lender be, I dig it. It's just I remember your rap at George's party. It's etched in my memory, to be honest ha ha. Ain't never heard anything quite like that, about native Americans and all. You must have done a lot of research and all, with your dates and battle descriptions and all, yet you came up with catchy riffs and hooks, and it ran over ten minutes, and you still got a whale of a reaction, and applause. They all wanted to hear more. Didn't Ariane ask you for your autograph? You got the gift, no doubt."

"Well, we'll see how this shakes out," said R., mollified. "Maybe after work one day."

"It'll happen one day," said Secret Hero dramatically.

"That's the spirit. I hope," R. replied. "Self expression and self realization are golden."

"By the way, what happened with that surgeon and you? I hear rumors."

"Turns out he did a competent job by all accounts. Will wonders never cease."

"You're doing a public service by making your complaint," Secret Hero asserted. "You may be lucky, but who knows how many other patients are out there. He shouldn't be drinking on the job. Good on ya. And remember, any time, give me maybe 72 hours heads up, and you have got a standing reservation at the studio."

"A time to every purpose under heaven," concluded R. "Later, Secret Hero."

The conversation with Super Hero triggered a flashback to George's graduation party. "Hey, hey, hey, look who the cat dragged in," George greeted him sardonically, his aviator glasses looming dangerously close to R's. sunglasses.

"I've seen the cat drag in a bird, and when I say "No" in a loud voice, the cat will drop the bird, and the bird will hop away, and live to fly another day," R. declared breezily, whisking by Cerberus, into rooms full of young people, talking and dancing, drinking and partying.

A big, phat bass pumped up the energy shaking the walls, vibrating the ceiling and floor. Marvin Gaye was singing,

Oh brother brother/we don't have to
oh sister sister
oh mother mother
oh father father we don't have to escalate.
What's going on? What's going on?

R. noted Leroi, the disc jockey, spinning tunes, who he met at a rave a few years ago. An eclectic, musical guy, if R. remembered correctly.

Walking among the dancing couples, R. slowly navigated towards the refreshments area, all kinds, tortillas, bean salad, tossed salad, salmon cakes, tuna croquettes, beer in kegs, Heineken, Dos Equis, Bass, Sam Adams, China beer, wines in many varieties, bottles aligned one after the other, and already, half-full, or quarter-full, Chinese dim sum, pretzel dips, on and on. R. helped himself to a salmon cracker and a glass of wine.

He surveyed the youthful scene. There was Jersey, chatting it up in a crowd, with the lithesome Ariane. R. had taken a psychology class with her at State a couple years before. Slender-hipped, thin-chested Ariane, with smoky hazel eyes, made a beeline towards him.

"Hi R.," she said tipsily, holding her glass of wine. "Did you come with Kimberly?" Ariane looked luscious and confused, in a pouty way. She wore tight blue jeans and a lavender tanktop with sequin sparkles. Heavy mascara lidded her catlike eyes, that seemed to moisten in his presence.

"Kimberley's here," R. replied. "There she is," R. pointed to a clique of partiers by a bedroom door.

"Wow, unsteady on my feet. This wine is overpowering me," said Ariane tipsily. "Take my arm will you, so I don't plaster my face on the floor."

Couples were smoking from bongs, getting high. Almost everyone seemed determined to cut loose, and get high, and make something happen, good or bad. The music played.

There's gonna be a party tonight
a party tonight I know,
there's gonna be a party tonight,
a party tonight I know…

R. grabbed hold of a second glass of wine, let his arm be taken by the shameless Ariane. They slithered and surried and boogied through myriad boogying couples, screaming and laughing and having fun. When they passed a large closet, R. impulsively dared Ariane, "wanna go into the closet and play spin the bottle. I'm in the closet you know."

Ariane grabbed his wrist and suddenly they were alone in a large closet, in the dark, rubbing up against coats and jackets.

"Where's the bottle, where's the spin?" Ariane inquired drunkenly, pulling R. close. She kissed him impulsively, flush on the lips. She felt lusciously sweet. Her perfume seemed intoxicating, and R. began to return her kisses heatedly, when his conscience, a small blue thing, edged between them, buried in the overcoats, as they were.

"Um, Ariane. Wow…You smell delicious." Another lip wrestling session seemed imminent.

Suddenly, three sharp knocks on the door, Jersey threw the door open and confronted them. "What have we here?" Jersey bellowed.

"We got lost on the way to the planetarium, and took refuge from the crowd," R. quipped and burst from the closet with alacrity, into the dining area. He began bopping to the music, munching on a tuna fish cracker, then started bopping towards Kimberly, wine glass in hand.

Kimberly—slender, heaving bosom, wine glass in hand, was debating heatedly with George, and a group of friends, against the near wall. The pumping bass made it all seem so cruel and surreal.

Jewels and binoculars hang from the head of the mule,
and these visions of Joanna make it all seem so cruel.

R. came up behind her, with a fresh glass of wine for him, for her. She took it from his hand, and gave him a big hug. "Having fun?" she asked. Her large, green eyes sparkled with magnetism and vitality. Her beautiful body swayed to the music.

"I am now," R. yelled, over the noise, with heartfelt sincerity. "I was beginning to lose hope…"

The group was debating national politics, and a candidates' debate. They were parsing the usual suspects, and taking sides. R. surveyed the scene, with drunken mien.

"Here we are, twenty-somethings or so, millennium kids mostly," R. murmured, "most of us totally broke, up to our ears in student loans, and working crap jobs, partying down like we're not stressed or fearful for the future." As if on cue a song came up.

So stressed out.
Remember the days when the Mama sang
and we imagined going to outer space,
Now we're all stressed out
and our friends say "get real,"
you got to make money.

R. worked on his second glass of wine, in and out of Kimberly's delicious arms. He couldn't take the political talk, so he tuned it out, and swayed to the music.

You can't hide your lying eyes
and your smile is a thin disguise.

Not true with Kimberly. He trusted her. She magnetized the moment he was in, with her vitality, her sheer presence, her decency, her sincerity. An hour or two went by. R. sampled the bong.

Somehow they got him over to the piano. He did not remember how. He launched spontaneously into a song he'd been practicing about Native Americans, smashmouthed drunk. It was about a group getting drunk in a gambling casino, and stumbling outside and receiving visions from their ancestors, who appeared as starmen and starwomen.

He couldn't remember really but a crowd of people gathered around the piano, and egged him on and cheered.

It was near the end by that time, and people began filing out the door.

Ariane tugged on his sleeve and said, "Can I have your autograph? You're going to be famous."

R. stuttered amid the sweaty bodies and stoned faces. "Hu-uh? You young lady are going to get home safely with a designated driver. Or you will be famous for all the wrong reasons. Promise?"

Ariane departed with Jersey. "I'm with him," she explained.

Kimberly came up behind him, and threw her hands over his eyes. The music with the pumping bass played on.

Coming right behind you, know I'm going to find you
one of these nights.

And they did. Later R. lay with Kimberly, feeling her heart beat. "They are just one more face in the crowd," R. realized, speaking aloud into the dark. "Kimberly and me, that's reality."

"Your breakfast is the most important meal of the day," Ms. Pike would announce emphatically to the children, before sitting them down to a nice, healthy breakfast. Kimberly remembered the Toast-ems, the scrambled eggs, the Coco Puffs, and a variety of other favorite cereals, the tall glass of orange juice, the camaraderie, the kidding. Arnold, eight years her senior, played rough sometimes, with nuggies and so on, but that was a big brother, that is what they do, she figured.

Kimberly remembered this, rather oddly, on a day when her mother invited her to sit with her, and have a "heart to heart."

At the same time, a little blond girl came running over to R., sitting on a park bench, and said "for you." She handed him a small, white card, with her sketch, a picture of a horse, or maybe a dog. "Aww, thank you," said R., but the little sprite had already run away.

Getting settled at the table, tea kettle whistling, Kimberly remembered climbing on the rocks in a rock garden in the park and her mother calling over, not hovering, "Kimberly, be careful."

"My only daughter," Mrs. Pike began. They were sitting in the well--appointed dining room, each with a piping hot cup of green tea. A carpet of leaves on the front lawn was being cleared by the Pike's yardman/ landscaper Manuel, and his assistant Jose.

Dolores Pike presented as perky, no-nonsense, bright-eyed and busy. Her hair was cut short in a blond bob, her features still pixie, even in her mature, middle age. She was 55.

"Did I ever tell you how I met your father?" Ms. Pike began.

"Of course, Mom," Kimberly replied, sipping her tee. "You guys met at the library—wait, no--or a rally or something, right?"

"Or something," Ms. Pike rejoined. "A group of us were sitting in at the Registrars. The Administration announced they were hiking tuition by 50% in the coming year. I was there on a scholarship with grants. However, there were girls in my suite who would have to leave school, or get a second, night job, to cover the increased tuition. Word went around and we organized a strike, a hunger strike. I was sitting on my butt, under a placard on the floor at the Registrars, with about 20 other students. In comes your father. He says he's concerned about our health, our strike being on Day 3 or so, gives a nice little speech. He takes our pulse, each of us, and goes around jotting the numbers on a piece of paper. He's worried about me, he says. He takes out a stethoscope, and asks 'may I check your heart?'"

"'No,' I said sharply. He smiled sheepishly, and went on his way. "A few students agreed to his exam."

"A week or so later, out of the blue, he calls me and asks me out on a date. I said 'yes.'"

"Later, I asked him how he got my number. 'Let's see,' he said, thinking about it. 'I was friendly with a student there. She knew your name. She remembered a list of students calling the protest, and the list included your name and number.' I laughed, like I could care less.

"Your father was vibrant, handsome, a young man with flashing white teeth, and a beautiful smile, when he relaxed and smelled the roses. He was in his first year of med school. The rest, as they say, is history.

Kimberly giggled. "I'm not sure I've heard that Mom. What a great story."

"I didn't know much about love, in retrospect," her mother said, a bit saucily. "I was a wide-eyed co-ed, intent on saving the world, or if not that, helping ease tuition rates anyway," she laughed. 'Yes, I was young once," she teased Kimberly.

Kimberly took the bait, in a fond way. "Mom, I know. I've seen the family scrapbook. You were a knock out."

"Whatever. Just so you know, my dear daughter. I remember the desire, the urge to surge."

Kimberly looked out the window. Jose had the infernal leaf blower blowing, barely audible from their cozy perch.

"I'm not nearly as good looking as you were," Kimberly admitted.

"What nonsense," her mother replied. "You're gorgeous. Everyone says it, everyone knows it. It's not easy being gorgeous. I'm proud of you, Kimberly. You're going to be a great nurse. You have integrity, and a good head on your shoulders, and willpower. Your grades win you honors."

"I don't know. Dad's heart episode scared the living daylights out of me. On top of R.'s car accident. The two men in my life KO'd in the space of a month. I felt devastated. I still do."

"Your father's doing fine, no worries," replied her mother. "He laughs like a kid each time he reads the sign on the fridge, 'No ice cream for Dad.'"

Suddenly, Jose was knocking on the door. "Ms. Pike could I talk to you? It's about the yard," Kimberly heard him say, in a heavy accent, while her mother stood with him by the door.

Her mother returned, after this brief interlude. "We needed to reset the sprinklers, for the time of year. Town water conservation guidelines and all," her mother announced. "Given the property taxes we pay, that is to say, an arm and a leg each year. So many responsibilities, duties to owning a house."

"Tell me about Richard," her mother switched gears suddenly, catching her off guard. "I want to hear."

"Well, he calls himself a drowned rat, a wounded cat," Kimberly began breezily.

"He's got issues," her mother responded. "Brilliant academically, but…"

"Volatile," Kimberly added. "Dynamic."

"Is it love?" her mother inquired gently.

"Love," Kimberly replied. "I can't help it."

"Tell me more," said her mother. She rose, and went to the kitchen, and put the kettle on.

"He is like a stray cat in a way," Kimberly gushed, with tears in her eyes, when her mother returned. "Is that bad?"

Her mother poured them each a new cup, and poured a little honey into each of their cups, with a little silver spoon.

"Is that bad?" echoed her mom. "You tell me."

Kimberly's confidence, in that moment, broke down, appeared a façade. But she recovered and proceeded boldly.

"I was just going along, taking my classes, to pick up my Biology degree. A relationship was not on my agenda at all. You remember the fiasco with Ron, when I was a sophomore. I felt like a fool! Did not want to even go there, was how I was feeling. Kinda bored, but doing okay. Mom, the moment I met him I felt something special. Like an electrical current passed between him and me. He came to the infirmary with a flu, and I was volunteering that day. I handed him a bottle of pills, an antibiotic.

"'Here, doctor says take these three times a day for seven days. Try not to go off schedule. If you miss a dose, very important, get back on the schedule right away. Take the whole seven day course, interrupting or stopping is a no-no,' I told him.

"He looked so under the weather, and exhausted. 'Thanks,' he said, and his eyes flashed with energy, and went liquid. He turned and walked out, coughing.

"A week or so later, he came by and told me his recovery was going well, would I have a cup of coffee with him? Yada yada.

"I felt an immense attraction. What can I say?" Kimberly left off, helplessly, shrugging her shoulders. "You know, he's a foster child. It hurts him. He feels like an outlier, an outsider. He's never experienced a family connection, an enduring one. Only temporary situations. I want to save him."

"Saving another person…very dicey," her mother admonished sternly.

"I want to marry him," Kimberly said impulsively.

Her mother sighed.

"Kimberly," she said warmly. "Did I ever tell you, we're related to the Bronte sisters on your father's side?"

"Really?," said Kimberly, surprised. "Weren't they writers?"

"They were. Sisters Charlotte, Emily, and Ann. I was an English major in college, you recall. When your father mentioned his family tree, it clicked in for me, that connection. A combination of factors of course, but I thought to myself, what a coincidence, the Bronte sisters are among my favorite authors."

Her mother paused. "Richard's been through so much lately. Jesus, when the D.A. called, I got frightened."

"Theater," Kimberly replied. "He was kidding."

"I have an idea," her mother laughed out loud. "What would you say if we have a party for him, a get-together at our house. Theater. We'll call it A Night of Music and Poetry at the Pikes, or some such."

"What's his full name?" Kimberly's mother wanted to know.

"Richard Rogers, you know," replied Kimberly. "Taken from one of his foster parents, he said."

"Richard Rogers, alright then. Good. We'll call it A Night of Music and Poetry Starring Richard Rogers, at the Pike Residence. How's that?"

"Umm. I don't know."

"Got a ring to it, doesn't it?," said her mother, warming to the project. "We'll do the hosting in a proper way. I'll handle all the arrangements, with you. We'll send out engraved, embossed invitations."

"Who will come?" Kimberly wondered, excitedly.

"Don't worry about who will come. Leave that to me," her mother promised.

"Well, can we invite our friends? He does have a few, though given his accident I think he's keeping a low profile, and focusing on healing for now."

--"Invite your friends, of course. Anyone you want," her mother affirmed, with enthusiasm. "The more the merrier. I hear he's quite a performer also. That song he performed over at George's party, a week or so before his accident, was quite a hit."

"How on earth…" Kimberly began.

"Never you mind. The walls have ears, so they say. Word gets around in a small town. Comes with the territory."

"Oh Mom," said Kimberly. "You're the greatest."

"Oh, a little party. A coming out party."

"You're the best," Kimberly gushed, and came round the table and gave her a big hug.

"He's an artist. A musician and a poet, I can feel it," Kimberly's mother concluded. "However, life is tough. That's not enough. He needs a way to make a living. There's the rub."

"Working on it," Kimberly responded. "At the party, after he sang his song, a girl asked him for his autograph, told him she thought he'd be famous someday."

"Anything's possible," said her mom. "But not likely."

"I know," said Kimberly. "I'll talk to him about this special night. He knocks me out with his art though. I can't go there, it's a wellspring, his wellspring."

"I want to show you, come," Kimberly's mother took her hand and led her to a closet in the master bedroom. "Way up high, on tippy toes, can you reach it?" Kimberly's mom pointed to a book on the top shelf, above the dresses and blouses, pants and slacks, baubles and necklaces.

Kimberly retrieved a large, brown book titled, *The Brontes,* by Brian Wilks. "My favorite book," Kimberly's mother exclaimed.

"Once a year maybe, I ask your father to take it down, and we spend an evening reading together. A biography of the Bronte sisters. With sketches by the sisters. Also, paintings by their brother, a talented portrait painter. Also, modern photos and from many years back showing the tourist attraction, around their house, the church, the graveyard, the heather. Great hardship in their upbringing, poverty, illness. Their father was an itinerant preacher, their devoted mother died from cancer in her ninth year of marriage. An 8 year old sister Maria, sent away to boarding school, contracted TB, and died. A second sister died from the same illness a few years later. The family was grief-stricken for years. They were very close. Liberal in a small village of conservatives. Their father encouraged the girls to read and write, they played games, contests, held writing nights at their house."

Kimberly sat down on the bed with her mother. They leafed through the book together, a few moments. "A spinning wheel, the house, the church, the graveyard, these sketches are awesome," Kimberly remarked enthralled.

"Life was hard," Kimberly's mother replied, gazing

at the pages with tears in her eyes. "Your father's ancestors," she reminded her daughter, with bright eyes. "Fortunately, your father's father worked for GE. He worked his way up the company ladder, and became a vice president. Made some wise investments also."

"Grandpa Carl..." Kimberly remarked, soberly. "So sad he passed away. I remember his funeral. I was in third or fourth grade."

"We have a few investments, honey," her mother said. "From Uncle Carl to you, your graduation gift, $50,000. Use it wisely okay?"

As if catching herself, Kimberly's mother hugged her. "You will," she said.

"I want to give this book to R., I'll return it soon enough?" Kimberly asked.

"Let R. have a look, of course," Kimberly's mom said. "Let him decide for himself if he's up for an evening of Music and Poetry Starring Richard Rogers, at the Pike Residence. If it's a go, good. Tell him to start rehearsing."

"I don't know about that," Kimberly asserted shyly. "He values spontaneity, that's where he shines."

"Whatever," said Kimberly's mother.

6

"Before we go let me put on my hearing aids. I forgot to put them on this morning."

Marge and Maida took the brief walk from the living room to the bathroom without their walkers. Marge tottered dangerously.

"In the bowl," Maida said.

"Huh?" Marge responded.

"You told me you keep them in the bowl," Maida reminded her loudly. "Batteries."

Marge began fiddling with two tiny metallic squares, with gnarled, arthritic fingers. "Almost," she cried. "Oh, these stupid things," she vented a cry of frustration.

"You don't need the bowl. Keep them in the cradle remember?" Maida reminded her.

"I don't know," said Marge.

Nurse Pike bustled in. "Marge, Maida, time for lunch dears. We'll see you in the dining room." Dolores Pike, Kimberly's mother had been working there many years. Among other things, she supervised the medications for more than 150 seniors.

"Dolores, help us," Maida implored. "Marge needs help with her hearing aids."

Dolores Pike popped the two batteries into the little cradles, waited a minute per instructions, and slide the cradles shut. “"Keep the batteries in their compartment, but open at night. Zinc likes the air, remember?" Nurse Pike repeated the litany.

"What cradle?" Marge rebuffed querulously. "Where's a cradle?"

Nurse Pike bent over Marge's translucent ears first her left, then her right, and installed the hearing aids.

"No cradle for me. I don't want them," declared Marge.

"You don't need to take them out, and put them in the bowl, that makes it more difficult for you later," Nurse Pike reminded her. "There you are, good to go."

"Marge, you're going loco," said Maida. "Come on, let's go to the dining room. I'm hungry already."

In the dining room a few minutes later, Marge and Maida joined 75 or so other seniors having their lunch. They filled out a menu, checking their selections. A few minutes later, a waiter served a chicken salad for Marge, and a tuna sandwich for Maida, with orange juice, and tea.

"Girls, ladies and gentleman," Nurse Pike made an announcement to the senior living community clients assembled for lunch. More were filing in by the moment, most seated, hunched over, grey, silver, fragile beings until recently able-bodied.

"Anyone here like music?" Nurse Pike inquired, in a booming, cheerful voice. "And poetry?"

"Yes," a few scattered assents and murmurs.

"I'm passing out invitations to each and every one of you. You are all invited to An Evening of Music and

Poetry at the Pike residence, my house. We're having a party. You're all invited."

She went table to table passing out embossed, engraved invitations.

"Anyone here like rap music?" A few groans went up. "No," a man called out.

"Well, young people will be performing. All different kinds of music, folk music, rock music, maybe rap music. Hope you'll consider trying something new. Art, culture, youthful energy, dancing. You would make a lovely audience.

"Also, my daughter will be there. I hope you all can make it. It will be fun. There's a sign up sheet by the front desk. Happy Bridges will be providing transportation for the evening, at no charge to you. You know, alittle culture, between the generations.

"Depending on the sign-up sheet, we'll plan the vans," Nurse Pike alerted

Josie, at the front desk, a few minutes later. "Could you alert the staff about the date and time, if anyone asks?"

"They'll love it," Josie responded enthusiastically. "A breath of fresh air away from here will do them good. They're always moaning about how they feel so cooped up. 'Why won't the vans take us for longer rides?' Or 'why won't my children come by, and take me for a ride?' I hear this every day. They feel neglected sometimes. This will be a nice break for them. By the way, can I go too?"

"Of course," Nurse Pike smiled. "The more the merrier. You could be their chaperone, if the scheduling works out."

7

R. drove up to the Pike residence in his Pontiac GT, under big, falling snowflakes. "A freshly falling silent shroud of snow," R. mused. "Appearances are deceiving. What kind of blanket, when a person who goes to sleep in it would die?"

R. gunned the engine one last time, ruminating on the snow, and strode into the Pike residence. In the hall, he hung up his coat, and not for the first time, admired the Victorian moulding, girls' smiling faces, that adorned the arches. Kimberly came to greet him, and wrapped her arms around his neck and gave him a long kiss. "Whatever happens this little soiree, I'll be with you at the end of the evening, promise," Kimberly said lightly, hands lingering on his shoulders.

"Oh, a little music and poetry night, what could possibly go wrong?" R. joked, leaning towards her and receiving a second kiss.

"The two most lovely ladies in the city, maybe the state," R. exclaimed histrionically, joining Kimberly and her mother in the dining room. They were setting out the victuals for the evening, on a long table, with a white tablecloth. The buffet included Greek salads, chicken salad, tuna on crackers, salmon croquets, many chips and dips, and also various bottles of wine. "Flattery will get you places," Ms. Pike rejoined. "Looks delicious," exclaimed R., innocently.

Outside, after awhile, cars began to pull up. The snowy suburban streets made a postcard backdrop for the arriving guests, filigrees forming along lamp posts, and in the garden, atop the architect-ed shrubs, that seemed so artistic and so finely wrought. "Manuel and Jose," thought R., "do a good job."

"Leroi should be here soon. He's liable to steal the show, get ready," R. joked, and cruised towards the living room to check out the staging area.

Dr. Pike was setting up a few chairs, and R. lent a hand, with alacrity. "Good God," he thought, "what a man, to invite me into his home, and let me put on a show. While I'm not even married to his daughter."

"Kimberly says you're feeling better, that's so important to her sir, and good to hear."

"Well, I am. No worries. You've been through it also? How goes with you?" A strong, kindly face beamed in his direction, but did not meet his eyes. "Doing well. Thanks to your daughter. Your daughter is a jewel."

Guestsbeganarrivinginwaves.GagglesofKimberly's classmates from nursing school sauntered in, and make straight for the wine coolers. "Is there any beer?" one inquires loudly. "In the fridge," Ms. Pike hollers back, from the other room. R.'s friends come following close behind, Connor with his girl Colleen, Peter, with a video camera, and Indiana Jones, with his girlfriend Sarah. R. went through an elaborate handshake with Connor, they devised way back in college, and perfected at the pinball factory, where they worked together for awhile. Hugs for Peter and Indiana, and their girl friends followed in close order.

"I'm going to video the event," Peter proclaimed. "For posterity. And for our future viewing pleasure. Sink or swim, smash or bomb, we'll have a record, and revise historically according to our whim, fashion, and mood at the time," Peter promised grandiosely. "After all, artists were born to revise, it's almost as important as creating."

"'Write in emotion, revise in tranquility,' a bard said," opined Indiana.

"Well, I see many a fair maiden over by the delectables, I wonder if they'd like to be in an independent movie?" said Peter enthusiastically. " Watch a master in action," he promised, and cruised over to the crowd of young ladies, who seemed pleased to hear his offer, and consider their next move, on camera.

"One more bounce, one more bounce, that client would not let me go," exclaimed Leroi, hanging up his coat, shaking hands all around with R., and Connor, Peter, and Indiana.

"Trouble at the studio?" Connor guessed.

"No trouble, just wanting a fatter bass, more bass, more bass, more bass. He's got three bad-ass versions now, and if the bass got any fatter, they'd have to scrape the fuzz off the walls," Leroi joked. "I'll set up over here," Leroi gestured to the north end of the living room, in front of the window. "Let's pull these curtains," and voila the vanilla chip curtains seemed a fine backdrop, barring the falling snow.

Leroi got busy with amps, and dials, and settings, and extention cords, for a Yamaha keyboard/synth that R. would play. The work went quick and easy, Leroi was a pro.

A commotion in the hall turned all their heads, and the Happy Bridges contingent made their way, many with walkers and wheelchairs, into the living room, amid cries of greetings and cheer. Carmella, their chaperone for the evening, was at pains to introduce everyone to everyone, in the vicinity, and explain the rules, and get the Happy Bridges guests seated, in a comfortable way, and with a plate in their laps.

R. sat down to tinker with the keyboard, and Leroi turned on the amp, and suddenly R. exclaimed "oh hell, I'm just gonna begin."

He launched into his song "The Wonderer." He looked like a muppet up there, fingers flying to the drum machine, Leroi on bass, getting it cranked up, and suddenly he was singing.

"Bob Dylan Lee Ann Rhymes drinkin' wine on the cross of time,
bigfoot Barberella sci-fi Cinderella, tears, idle tears, but faith
grows through the years, serenity when many are stumblin', devotion
when many are fumblin'. Electricity leaps from Madonna's face a
cougar's magnetic grace electricity purrs in the bones of her face
oh oh magic kingdom place in another time and place love's body state of
grace a wave of hair a different face…"

Peter tore himself away from the girls and rushed in with the video rolling.

Many girls took their seats, while many others remained standing around and about, against the wall, and by the door, sipping alcoholic beverages, swaying their hips, getting soused.

R. nursed a glass of wine, situated by his right foot, by the reverb pedal. The evening proceeded apace.

singing 'here's a soul invitation my part is inspiration may your spirit
follow me in time dance to the music drink the wine yeah yeah a nickel
and dime nickel and dime nickel and dime. sound the bells of rimney
the missing iron chime sound the bells of rimney oh in the fullness of
time in another time and place love's body state of grace in another
time and place love's body state of grace.

A smattering of applause. Didn't matter. R. was just getting warmed up.

"Here's a song I'd like to dedicate to my one, my only, Kimberly," R. proclaimed.

When I look into your bedroom eyes when I look into your bedroom
eyes when I look when I look into your bedroom eyes when I look into
your bedroom eyes.

Just last night I had a dream, two stars falling from the sky, landed
on earth and there they were when I looked into your bedroom eyes.
When I first saw you I got high as a kite, when you put your arms
around me I knew we would be alright. Take this longing I have that
comes on so strong, take this pride that sometimes gets in the way,
we've come and we've gone to where words have no tongue,
speak to me with your bedroom eyes, speak to me with your bedroom eyes.

Applause. Sounded sweet to his ear. Someone shouted out,"kite." Or did they say "kike"?

R. plunged on, with a rap about the Bronte sisters, that R. composed, inspired by the book Kimberly turned him on to, that she had borrowed from her mother.

"This is to Ms. Pike, and Kimberly, and Dr. Pike, whose family tree goes back to the Bronte sisters, very distinguished indeed, and I see the family resemblance," R. joked. "That splendid jaw."

Much laughter.

R. did his Muppet thing at the keys while belting out the song.

Nearer to God oh yeah,
the church, graveyard and sod, oh yeah,
looming over them, right next door.
Charlotte, Emily, and Ann

had each other and their dad,
they did not want for more.

He taught them how to read,
after they tended the chicken feed,
also, taught them well how to write.
To the conservative town
girls reading and writing down
did not set right.
The Bronte sisters really cut loose
on a double standard, social abuse,
they put their life and times down in a book,
and charmed society to take a second look,
they helped fuel the train, they worked hard as any man,
but they were always kept in the caboose,
kept in the caboose, kept in the caboose.

"Not finished yet, a work in progress," R. snarled to much applause.

"Now I'd like to introduce Leroi, who I'm proud to call my friend, DJ extraordinaire, producer, songwriter, and performer, who will do a little rap for you."

"America, where the cops accost you arrest you, and put
you in a chokehold, for standing on the sidewalk,
smoking a cigarette, and being asthmatic, then hustle
you into their death car, where you ride and come out dead,
who's the gangster now?
America, where the cops stop you for riding a bicycle
because of the color of your skin, and the time of night,
and shoot you full of holes, because your i.d. is in your pocket

and you reach for your i.d.
who's the gangster now?
America, unlike Europe, where there's universal
healthcare, where only due to obamacare do 25 million
have health insurance so if they get cancer, they have
a chance to be cured.
who's the gangster now?
America, where if you're walking down the street
and black, and you have outstanding parking tickets,
and the cops call you to stop, and you keep walking,
they may shoot you in the back 40 times, and be excused.
who's the gangster now?

"Give him the hook," a man called out. It was Stanley from the Happy Bridges group.

"Why the hook"? Leroi responded. "Are you scared to hear the truth? Black lives matter."

"What about black on black crime, write a song about that," Stanley rejoined.

"Maybe I will," Leroi answered. "But now I'm writing a song about this. Do you feel threatened? How would you like to wake up one morning and hear your son had been gunned down by police due to the color of his skin."

"Wouldn't like it!" Stanley admitted. "You got me there."

"Alright," said Leroi. "The point is it's not black vs. white, it's wrong vs. right."

"Sir, Leroi," Carmella raised her hand. "Isn't it true these police are being put in jail for their crimes?"

"Every so often," Leroi replied. "Not enough though.

Many of them walk. You know, the D.As. Goes against their grain to prosecute their own."

Ms. Pike came to the fore, and clapped her hands. "Wasn't that terrific? So much passion, and emotion. We're all alittle sweaty," she joked. "Let's take a break. Have an intermission. R. and Leroi will be back in a few minutes. How about a big round of applause for R. and Leroi?"

They received a nice round of applause. The murmurs and conversation turned heated and excited. The evening had turned towards the provocative.

Carmella waded into the Happy Bridges crowd. "How's everyone doing?" she inquired cheerfully. "Okay," one said. "Exciting," said another. "Where's the poetry?" said a third. "Bathroom," said a lady in a wheelchair.

(It was Marge.)

"Are you having a good time Marge?" Carmella asked, navigating her chair towards a bathroom.

"No," said Marge. "Too noisy."

"Would you like me to turn down the volume on your hearing aid?" inquired Carmella solicitously.

"Yes," said Marge. Carmella stood over her in the hallway, fiddling near her ear.

"No," Marge said," it's alright. Bathroom. Hurry."

Carmella helped her out of her chair, onto the toilet seat. She shut the door. "I'm done," Marge cried, a few minutes later.

"Hurry," Marge exhorted. "I want to get back."

"You like it," Carmella declared. "Do you want me to turn down the volume? You have three settings remember?" No reply, so Carmella bent over her, removed the hearing aid, and reset the volume.

"No," Marge said, as R. launched into his next number. "I want it louder." Carmella settled Marge next to Maida, who sat in a folding chair.

"If it gets too loud, pull, take your hearing aid out," Maida said disgustedly.

"This one's called 'American Dreamer,' R. announced. "It starts in a mysterioso minor chord riff, and...

Johnny's got a heavy job working in a grocery
lifts 5o lb. boxes to the top row,
George is workin' sponges in a car-wash,
hops hot cars down in Soho.
If you wanna call this a coming of age song
it's alright, alright, alright,
Danny says, 'I'm an American dreamer,'
give em the day, take back the night,
give em the day, take back the night.

Loretta works for a florist,
sends bouquets to her friend half price,
Joni's an airline stewardess,
flies the New York-to Paris-to Hong Kong flight.
If you wanna call this a coming of age song
it's alright, alright, alright,
Joni says, 'I'm an American consumer, that's right,'
give em the day, take back the night,
give em the day, take back the night.

Before the last chord died away, a voice shouted out, "I'll sue you for using my name in your song." It was George. Was George invited?

R. ignored him. He was already singing, banging the keyboard like a muppet. He played it many times, to complete silence.

"Come all without, come all within,
you've not seen nothin' like the mighty Quinn."

"Ha ha, not my song, I like that one," R. confessed. A smattering of applause.

"Here's a song about a little bird, that's flying from the nest the first time."

Arrow, snares and nets, there are many turns
many will get lost, in a land where they will burn
or give in to the freezing cold, or settle in a cage of gold,
or lands of silver that hold no desire.
Ooh, fledgling bird, flying through the sky alone
your song has the sweetest tone, your mother's heard
fledgling bird.

There's traps and bows, the hunter's song you've heard
what's a mother to do, but sing like a bird, do do do.
Ooh, fledgling bird, flying through the sky alone
your song has the sweetest tone, you're almost home
fledgling bird.

"Sweet guitar work, great touches this one got some great progressions and R. gives it. Finds his niche here on this one. Steely Dan, groovin' on the flute, and the guitar work and doo doo then that little break in the middle of the song is a piece of genius coolness. But really gotta love the guitar work. Killer vibe…" Peter proclaimed. He did not care who heard.

"That's a synth for ya. Guitar, flute, got it all, helps independent music spread the word" replied R., before launching into his next song.

When lilacs last in the dooryard bloomed, the civil war was done,
the Southland had surrendered, the Union held, and won,
after all the bloodshed, a new morning had begun,
the President went to the theater, met the jealous son.

Son of the Confederacy said "please allow me,
to introduce myself," in an irony,
shook the President's hand, played with Lincoln's boy,
debonair at small talk, his honey tongue employ.

"I'm Booth the actor," he declared, "the most famous in the land,"
Booth chatted up the first lady, talked about gardening,
the way Brutus dispatched Caesar, Mary was impressed,
and with the headlines stapled to his chest.

When lilacs last in the dooryard bloomed, Lincoln was alive and well,
his funeral train crosses the nation, like a long black veil,
from a boy in a log cabin, to a dinner date,
the man who saved the union, saved the United States.

Lincoln never saw it comin', the lion uncaged,
shouts "thus the tyrant dies," and leaps on history's stage.

Were the authorities bribed to look the other way?
In the mist of history, unclear to this day,
a full moon risin', blowin' in the breeze,
one guard for the President snores, he was catchin' zzzs.

A couple weeks later Booth was dead and gone,
the man who killed the president, they caught him in a barn,
a week or so after, they caught his accomplices,
hustlers, thieves, ex-soldiers, known to the local police.

"It's getting very near the end," R. joked. "I enjoy writing songs about U.S. presidents. When I was back in foster homes, I thumb-tacked a chart of the U.S. presidents to my wall. When I went to a new foster home, which was every year or so, I'd roll the chart up, and thumb-tack it onto the wall of my next room, first thing. Gave me a sense of continuity anyway, slender though it was." This is called "Jefferson's Expedition."

R. sat down at the keyboard, and here Leroi came up and adjusted a few knobs on the board, while R. began to play pulsing organ riffs.

Sent Lewis and Clark on their expedition,
opened up the west, open to diversification,
explored Washington and Oregon during my administration,
what democracy could create in these United States.

My fist wife Martha died, her golden worth,
our children but one perished in childbirth,
what I cherished turned to dust, returned to earth,
like hit by a freight train running through the United States.

Sally Hemmings got a raw deal,
she would ask me "how does it feel?"
¾ white, by law a slave, we helped each other heal,
like on a blind date in the United States.

United we stand, divided we fall,
wrote the Declaration of Independence for all,
people responded with a battle call,
revolution couldn't wait in the United States.

"Awesome concert man, top notch, you're going to be famous," Peter said enthusiastically, in the kitchen, throwing a towel over R.'s sweating face.

"The Champ," he says.

"No," says R. "a dark horse on a dark course at best, but thanks for the towel." R. laughed at the thought, "a hundred thousand other indie musicians out there playing their hearts and souls out for peanuts, been there before me, do not see it happenin' bro," R. replied. "A happy thought tho."

"I videotaped it, for all to see. Either way, you're a part of history now."

Connor and Indiana came up, slapping R. with high 5s, and congratulating him on his performance, his playing, and his songwriting skills. "I was totally enthralled," Indiana said. "You had me from the first song. I wanted to hear more."

"Leave 'em wanting more, R., isn't that the saying, and you did," Connor added warmly.

Kimberly came in and gave R. a big hug. "You rehearsed," she said.

Behind Kimberly followed George. "R., I gotta say, it wasn't as painful as my dentist. Almost, but not quite," George mocked.

The room fell silent. Kimberly stepped gingerly over a spilled beverage, on second thought, gave it a swipe, and said "I'll be in the living room, helping my mom clean up."

"Aw, pay him no heed, he's just jealous," Connor quipped, giving Indiana a gentle elbow, and popping open a bottle of water. Connor took a big, long sip.

"Jealousy, that mocks the meat it feeds on," quoted Indiana. "Guess we got it bad George, eh?"

"George, who looked flushed and drunk, turned a fiery red. "I'm going to talk to Kimberly," he replied haughtily, and walked out.

"Catching any musical waves lately?" inquired Indiana. "Independent music seems to be booming."

"Booming and busting," responded R. "Your song could be streamed 1,000,000 times and that will get you about $100 on Spotify or Pandora. Music buyers are down 50% from a decade ago. Why buy, when you can get your music for free? Maybe, if you're lucky, selling t-shirts at a concert will put you in the black, after you have a following, and thousands of hours of touring and work. That's about it," said R. "Everyone wants to be famous."

"It's not right," said Indiana.

"Anyhoo, that Blurry Faces song about stress, and a song "Ship to Wreck" I heard today on the radio, that's primo stuff."

"'Ship to Wreck,' I heard that," Indiana replied. "Girl's got a grand, soaring vocal, bells and whistles production, and lyrics that go deep. 'There's a great white shark in my bed, there goes a killer whale/am I losing touch/did I drink too much/did I build this ship to wreck?' A good, pointed question," said Indiana.

"Well, did you?" Connor asked R.

A pregnant pause. "I dunno," R. admitted. "I hope not. Too soon to tell."

"You have a co-pilot now, don't blow it on hollow dreams, backwater and backdraft," Connor teased.

"Took me years to understand this body is a gift from millions of years ago, millions of years in the making, that my soul inhabits, and a fine temple it is," noted Indiana. "Respect your earthly condition, and situation. Don't pollute your temple, or minimize pollution anyway."

"Spoken like a true ecological freak," joked George, reentering the room and entering the conversation, looking for trouble, with a florid, drunken mien.

"Doesn't matter that you're on Law Review or whatever, doesn't matter that you're interning for a big corporation," Indiana teased. "Kimberly wants Richard, not you. Must be hard to swallow, eh?" he said sharply.

"You little pissant," George exploded. "What do you know? Go film an avante garde urination festival."

"And you," George continued to Connor, "go paint a house."

"Ooh the big reveal, when the beast slinks out. Shows his true colors, ouch that hurt," Connor rejoined.

"You, you…"

"You, you…" Connor replied. Peter and Indiana laughed. "Ho ho ho, take a look in the mirror. Get him to the vet," Indiana cried.

"Go drink a bottled water, hope it's from a poisoned well," George practically spit at Indiana. "I'm going to be a corporate attorney. Just you wait. I'll be laughing."

Kimberly heard his last remark and said, "George, if you're gonna major in obnoxious, make like a tree and leave."

"Punk ass music, radical friends, who needs them?" he fumed. "Who are you, the three wisemen come to meet the radical Savior?" he said vehemently.

He departed the room, fuming. He slammed the front door on his way out.

8

"How would you like to go to Asia? Thailand? China?" R. proposed.

"Huh? What are you talking about?" replied Kimberly.

"To save a tree going extinct?" replied R.

"Are you kidding?" Kimberly said skeptically. "Tell me."

"Received a letter from my friends in Thailand, Ivan and Lisa. They're going."

"To help save an extinct tree?"

"Well, they're already there in Thailand. They stumbled on a professor and her research group, at a fly-by-night airport or something, got to talking, the professor explained about her project. Saving a tree threatened with, and in danger of extinction?"

"Like our relationship?" Kimberly responded.

R. looked across the room, shocked for a moment. Taken aback.

"Kimberly," he cried. "What are you saying? That wounds."

Tears came to R.'s eyes. "I'll go crazy. I want to kill myself."

Kimberly walked over, with misty eyes. "I was kidding silly." She sat down next to him, and put her hands on his shoulder.

"I intended to say, or make a comparison, is all. We have a rare relationship. We're like two rare trees, entwining. In a modern world, that seems intent on neutering growth, and rendering growing a dangerous activity. Sorry," she explained.

"'Two hearts, beating with one mind.' Like the song goes?" R. wavered, fearful and uncertain.

"Don't worry," Kimberly repeated. "The wolf is always at the door, my love. Perhaps—you know—we should think about our future together. Very carefully. Exchange rings, and stuff. Anyway, tell me more about Thailand?"

"They need assistants. To help with the research, help plant new trees. Help enter data on their computers. The whole nine yards. Ivan and Lisa are on board, and recommended us, if we want to go."

"Oh my god. When?"

"Next summer maybe? Ivan and Lisa are on the scene now, and having a great time, they say. They are in these remote forests in Thailand, digging up roots, taking samples every day. The professor's returning in a few weeks to the States. However, she plans on raising funds for a return project to Thailand this summer, to initiate a second phase, or whatever. Planting the seeds, in the right places, from what Ivan gathers. Stuff like that."

"Saving a nearly extinct tree. Wow. I love it," Kimberly replied. "Does the tree have a name?"

"Let's see, it says here." R. strode over to his notebooks

and leafed through until he found the email from Ivan. "The Chinese cypress?" responded R., from memory. "The Chinese cypress," he said reading carefully Ivan's note.

"That's so cool," replied Kimberly enthusiastically.

"It's because of my scars" said R. stoically.

"Oh Richard my dear," Kimberly replied, "Come sit down with me."

Kimberly sat on the bed, and patted the space beside her, for him to sit. He walked over to her fearfully, like a child. Suddenly, he felt very uncertain, and insecure.

"I'm sorry," R. cried. "I'm a mess." He began weeping on her shoulder.

Soon large tears were flowing from his eyes, and wetting Kimberly's blouse. Tears fell like rain.

Kimberly held him, while he went through spasms of crying.

"Shh, shh," Kimberly consoled. "You've had it tough, you've looked into the abyss. God knows how I would deal with what you've been through. Probably, go hide in my parents' house, and never come out. I know, I know," she commiserated. "But all that's over now. The bruises on your face are starting to fade. Your hair is growing out, over the sutures. No one could tell you've been in a car accident a few short months ago."

"But my lip," R. confessed, "is still numb, on the left side. Look at my chest," he exclaimed, lifting his shirt for her to see. There were visible scars, and burn marks.

"This will heal, the doctors say," Kimberly reminded him. "Your lip looks fine from the outside, the numbness will fade, they say, remember? It feels funky, I know. A couple of my girlfriends got botox injections recently. They go on and on about the numbness. 'They came so far for beauty,'" she joked.

R. sniffled. "Kimberly."

"Yes, Richard."

"If a certain guy loved a certain girl, and wanted to ask her an important question."

Kimberly met his lips with hers, in the quiet ambiance. Kimberly pulled herself away for a moment, to turn off the lamp. R. sat slumped, dejected, depleted. "Let's lay down," Kimberly suggested, gently cradling him in her arms. Slowly, they began kissing, finding each other, like for the first time.

They went on a long journey, drifting in and out of lifetimes. Though the cars passed by outside, and tv sounds from the other room, they made love all through the night, and left a few fear images behind, temporarily anyway.

They rose together the next morning, and did not say much. Kimberly needed to rush off to a 9 o'clock class. Kimberly prepared the scrambled eggs, and R. fixed the high fiber cereal, Heart To Heart, with extra toppings of strawberries and green grapes, along with juice and coffee for them both.

"I like the name," R. mused.

"Yeah," Kimberly agreed.

They stood at the door, and kissed. "There are 23 year olds who talk about fashion statements with oversized handbags, and can't bear waiting for the next episode of Game of Thrones. That's not me. I'm in it for the long haul," said Kimberly.

"Moi aussi," said R. "My dear love, we'll talk. See you later."

"Bottles bottles everywhere and not a drop to drink," joked Ms. Pike, the next afternoon, cleaning up with Kimberly.

"How much wine, how much beer?" exclaimed Kimberly. "Quite a lot."

"The Happy Bridges folks loved the carrot cake," Kimberly's mother declared. "Guess if they got this far, their genes genie are okay with the sweets every now and then. Constitutions like iron, some of them. Marge and Maida are probably in their 90s, 100 is doable these days, they may make it, maybe."

Kimberly assembled the bottles in a row. "To the recycling bin," she declared, lugging them out two at a time, rather than risk mingling them in a garbage bag and breaking a few.

Ms. Pike attended to the dirty forks and spoons, the scores of dirty paper plates.

"Look," said Ms. Pike, when Kimberly returned to the living room. She pointed at the fallen banner she had created, A Night of Music and Poetry at the Pike Residence. "Reminds me of Jurassic park, at the end" she said drily.

Kimberly giggled. "That's funny, Mom."

"A big success, I'd say," said Ms. Pike cheerfully. "Everybody was yakking and smiling and laughing while they departed, an animated bunch, from what I could see. That's a good thing. We could use more culture in our lives, around this town. We should do this again next year, if not sooner."

"Great, Mom. Richard cut loose, I think it was really good for him. His friends are really there for him. They think he's a genius, or something."

"I don't know," said Ms. Pike. "Like Shakespeare. Or Dante?"

"They are into the music scene, they know what's what, and when they hear quality, they'll say so, and they pull no punches. They would not be shining him on, blowing smoke up his behind, they're too passionate about music for that."

"Well, a talented lad, for sure," Ms. Pike declared warmly. "Maybe he'll form a band and take his show on the road."

"He really likes teaching. Getting his feet wet, substitute teaching, mostly English, but he also qualifies in history, and math. It's a revelation he says. A new world."

"They need new worlds to conquer, or explore anyway," Kimberly mother replied. "They want to carve out their niche, quest, go on great adventures. At their best, they spur us women on to follow, and we do."

"Well, I'm not a follower," said Kimberly saucily.

"A follower may be a good thing," said Ms. Pike. "We all need nurturing, encouraging, validation, affirmation. Time passes. Often the follower becomes the leader."

"Well, I'm getting plenty of volatility and unpredictability for sure," Kimberly replied. "But underneath it all, after all is said and done, he needs me to help guide him on his great adventure. I feel that," said Kimberly, "I'm the pilot also."

"You are dear," Ms. Pike replied. "My child's a pilot.

You will never understand your man fully. Relationships have mystery, like the air we breathe. It's a touch of strangeness, otherness, amid the familiarity, what-we think-we-know, that keeps us on our toes. Hold on loosely and don't let go, if you cling too tightly, one loses control."

"You and Daddy did it."

"We work on it every day. It never ends," Ms. Pike replied.

"God, Mom, observing the Happy Bridges folks walk outside to their vans, in the snowy night, they reminded me of nude, bent trees in the winter breeze. Does it all have to end so sad?" Kimberly wondered.

"They've led full, rich lives most of them. That's what you do not see. They've enclosed so much life. It's in their blood. 'A time to every purpose under heaven.'"

"Yeah," Kimberly replied. "A time to every purpose under heaven. Stages on life's way. I forgot."

"You're right," Kimberly's mother rejoined, "it's sad." She gave her daughter a big hug, and looked around the room. "Clean up time is done," she declared with satisfaction. "So much for A Night of Music and Poetry at the Pikes," and they both laughed.

9

R. drove down broad suburban streets, away from his apartment complex, down towards a commercial/residential district on the other side of town. Leroi's studio shared a building with Construction Wreckers, and R. parked next to a giant black pick-up truck on one side, and a dump truck on the other side.

"From these humble beginnings," R. joked to himself, "comes the new wave. Music that will scratch the face of eternity. Or not."

Leroi's production skills were in demand. Rock, pop, rap, funk, gospel, country, all kinds of musicians utilized his services. He had a rep as a skilled producer, and at reasonable rates.

"Yo, dog," Leroi greeted R., ushering him into the studio. He was a tall, muscular, African American guy with close-cropped hair and a friendly smile. "You missed my prior client Avery by a couple of minutes. He's an interesting guy. Does rock music basically with jazz flavorings. Keeps it moving. Works as a flight attendant for Jet Blue. The guy can really play." Leroi liked to keep his clients plugged in, informed, every so often they'd strike a spark, do collabros. The power of networking.

"Whatever," said. R., sniffling, with a sharp cough.

"Dude, are you alright for a vocal tonight? You shouldn't sing if you're under the weather."

"I'm alright," replied R.

"Hey, after that performance the other night, which was killer, maybe you're paying the price with a cold. Gotta pay you know," Leroi joked.

"It was alright?" R. wondered.

"Are you kidding? Get a band together, man. Take it on the road. You've got velvety vocal tones. That don't hurt. Your lyrics are subterranean, complex, imagist, and you're a fine storyteller. Cool piano playing, up there with Elton John yuck yuck. Audition a few guys. Start with clubs. You could do it."

"I dunno," R. replied.

"Dig the history songs too. They're unique. Never hear songs like that. Maybe a bit like the song Secret Hero and I are working on, about 'I Have A Dream.'"

"You think so?" queried R. "Maybe a bit of client petting going on," thought R. But basically, he liked Leroi, seemed straightforward enough. Anyway, tonight's session was on Leroi, per his invitation, and R. figured they would sound each other out, and take it from there.

"So what's on the menu tonight?" Leroi prepped him.

R. picked up a guitar and strummed. "A song about Tom Paine," said R.

"Rings a bell," said Leroi. "Didn't Dylan do a song about him, a song called "Tom Paine"?

"Good memory. Way back there in the 60s. Mentions him in the title, but not about Tom Paine at all."

"Alright, alright, 'Tom Paine.'"

R. played him the song on guitar.

Could have served ol King George
could have served the Crown,
his heart beat warmer
in the cold New England town.
Ben Franklin came in one morning
John Adams the next,
they talked about human right,
while he ran his printing press.
These are the times that try men's souls,
these are the times,
let em roll,
time'll tell, says Tom Paine.

"Alright, alright, a history song. Dig it. That's where the bodies are buried," Leroi responded.

R. strummed, and sang the next verse.

Says Tom, 'we should shine together
we should carry the torch,
democracy should light the way
or likely we'll be scorched.
The sun also rises,
the birds do sing,
across our country
let the chimes of freedom ring.
These are the times that try men's souls,
these are the times,
let em roll,
common sense makes sense,' says Tom Paine.

'Torched/scorched', like that, haven't heard that before. Like the change up in the chorus. Keep going," Leroi encouraged.

John Adams said George Washington's sword
might have been in vain,
if not for the golden hand,
the fountain pen of young Tom Paine.
Napoleon says he kept
Tom's book under his pillow,
the little dictator fooled him
with wine au portabello.
'These are the times that try men's souls,
these are the times,
let em roll,
'no gain without pain,' Tom Paine.

"You pun there, in the last verse. 'Pain/Paine', I like that. Changes up the chorus again, check. In a mystery key, E minor. I'm hearing a solo, should be nice playing off that pretty, mysterioso melody. Kind of plaintive, gypsy emotion there. Want to do a click? Are you ready maestro?" Leroi urged.

"Ready when you are. Let's get a tempo."

Leroi sat down, and clicked the mouse a few times, the drum program already on the screen. They tried this, and tried that…

"A ballad, but upbeat, not mournful, hopeful," R. commented.

A little give and take, here and there, and they had a tempo. R. played the song through, to the metronomic, draft beat. Sounded natural enough, if only temporary, Leroi would lay down a proper drum track during the week.

R. excused himself and popped the fridge in the next room, and drank a bottle of water. R. noticed honey sitting on the shelf. He poured himself a spoonful of honey, and returned to the recording session.

"Ready to do the rhythm guitar?" Leroi inquired.

"Let's do it." They miked the guitar, and away R. played.

They did the guide vocal next. Usually a draft, but every so often, the guide vocal stuck. R. nailed a good one on the first try. The honey helped.

Done. They had taken two hours. Now came the production end. What instruments to accompany the simple rhythm guitar and vocal.

"Hear a cello in the solo definitely, bring out the gypsy passion. These were mostly farmers and small businessmen fighting the mighty British Empire. They were risking everything in order to throw off the yoke of tyranny."

"Yeah, unfair taxes, a foreign army in their midst, being treated like servants, or second class citizens by the British. I dig the American revolution. The Declaration of Independence, 'all men are created equal.' I dig it," opined Leroi, the advocate.

"That's right," said. R. "They were fed up and were not going to take it anymore."

"It's in the books," said Leroi. "Even if it was white men."

"Like you said the other night Leroi, 'it's not black versus white, it's wrong versus right.'"

"Depends whose ox is being gored," rejoined Leroi. "Yeah, that's a dope song, could apply to any of us. Let's play around with it."

The "fun" part, playing around with percussive sounds, clay drums, bongos, shakers, tambourines, til they felt satisfied, got the feel of it, proceeded.

"Next week then," R. stood by his car.

Leroi would lay down a proper drum track, and a bass track, in the interim, probably in the next few days. "Tuesday, 6:30 sharp, that'll be our time," Leroi reminded him. Next week they would work on the production, R. was looking forward to tackling the cello part.

R. departed, gingerly easing his car out between the dump truck and the humongous pick up, with a few early "bounces" in hand, that he listened to on his car CD player, driving home. He nodded and bopped in time to the music. Next week he'd lay down the piano track also, it mainly being a piano song, he decided.

His song "Tom Paine" was busy being born, like a fetus, in vitro, developing, evolving, preparing to meet the world.

R. moved his head along to the rhythms and cadences, slapped the dash with his spare hand keeping time, hearing parts evolving in his head.

He wanted to see Kimberly, he called her from his car.

All of a sudden, lights start flashing in his rear view mirror. He hears a couple of quick bursts from a siren, a police car behind him.

"Oh great," R. muttered, "now what? I'm not

speeding, only going 35 or so in a 40 mile per hour zone, did not blow through any stop signs…"

R. went to roll down his window, which he did so infrequently it took him a few seconds to find the button.

The officer stood outside his window, on a cold winter night, blowing vapors on the glass. "The gods of winter," R. murmured. Finally the window rolled down. "License and registration please."

"What's the problem, officer?"

"Wait," he said. The officer strolled back to his car.

A few minutes later he walked back, with R.'s papers.

"You look familiar," the officer said.

R. gulped. "Not on any wanted posters," R. quipped, and immediately regretted it. How could he be so stupid, to joke around and be flip in this situation?

The officer took off his gloves.

"Sorry, Officer. A little nervous, I guess."

"Aren't you the kid in the car accident a few months ago?" the officer inquired, studying his profile.

"Yes," R. replied. "Near the detour on Route 6."

"You cheated death," the officer declared, motioning with R.'s paper, then holding back. "You were lucky you were thrown from the wreck before the car exploded."

"I don't remember," said R.

"Well, let's imagine you're a cat with nine lives. How many lives do you think you have left?"

"I don't know," responded R. "I don't want to know."

"You're clean," said the officer, handing R. back his paperwork through the open window. R. could sense his breathy vapor trail. R. looked ahead anxiously.

"Your left tail light's busted," he informed R. "Get it fixed as soon as possible." R. promised he would.

The officer walked back to his car, and drove away.

PART 3

10

"Science is a quest to free ourselves from the chains of superstition and wrongheaded thinking. No more! Medicine, similarly, is a journey through ignorance towards knowledge. Information is power, a cliché but true."

"The history of medicine is fraught with erroneous assumptions, and wrong turns. To err is human. It is how we respond to our errors and setbacks that marks a person's character and resolve. Science maintains that we may learn from our mistakes, make progress. Similar to a student at school, such as yourselves, going over a quiz, perhaps on this very topic, and learning from your mistakes, so the next time the question comes up, you will have the correct answer."

A few titters. That made them sit up and take notice. "Learning by trial and error, that is often what it takes."

Kimberly slipped into the back of the lecture hall at UConn State Med School, to hear her father speak. One of her nursing courses was covering infections, and here was her father, a professor at a med school, discoursing on a closely related topic.

She did not want to embarrass him, or make him

nervous, so she sat unobtrusively in a red hoodie, prepared for taking notes. R.'s appreciation of her father caused her to value him more dearly than ever. "Don't take him for granted," she would remind herself. She was just starting out on a career journey and he had completed the circuit.

"Today we'll discuss briefly a few pioneers in the history of medicine. Each made significant breakthroughs. Louis Pasteur, Robert Koch, Richard Ross, Walter Reed, and Alexander Fleming."

A student raised her hand. "A child bit by a rabid dog, who was foaming at the mouth, contracted rabies."

"Very good," Dr. Pike responded warmly.

"To save a child's life, Pasteur worked feverishly to create a vaccine, a weakened, attenuated version of the disease, to train our immune system, our antibodies, to recognize the invading disease cells as enemies, and to fight them in the future. That is how a vaccine works.

"Pasteur created vaccines before people recognized that germs could cause diseases. They thought he was mad basically, or a charlatan, a fraud.

"Boohooed by the doctors of his day, Pasteur led the way to the acceptance of vaccines over the course of his life, despite determined resistance by skeptics in the medical profession and the generally ignorant.

"Light versus darkness. Verifiable and repeated experiment versus vague theories and sheer poppycock. That is how Pasteur prevailed.

"Saving millions of lives in the process. Anthrax, a new vaccine. Rabies, new vaccine.

"Louis Pasteur, a French chemist and microbiologist

renowned for his discoveries of the principles of vaccination, microbial fermentation and pasteurization.

"How about Robert Koch? Ring a bell anyone?"

No hands were raised.

"Not quite a household name, is he? But his research and discoveries saved millions of lives. Tuberculosis, also known as consumption, attacked the lungs, victims coughed up blood, and slowly withered away. As the founder of modern bacteriology, he is known for his role in identifying the specific causative agents of tuberculosis, cholera, and anthrax and for giving experimental support for the concept of infectious disease. In addition to his trail-blazing studies on these diseases, Koch created and improved laboratory technologies and techniques in the field of microbiology, and made important discoveries in public health. D. H. Lawrence, John Keats, The Bronte sisters, Robert Louis Stevenson, possibly Edgar Allen Poe, possibly Ralph Waldo Emerson, all died of tuberculosis. The list goes on and on.

"How about Richard Ross?"

No one raised their hand. "Not a household legend," Dr. Pike joked. "Ross, a lowly researcher in India, discovered the etymology of malaria, that was killing millions worldwide each year. How a parasite infects a mosquito, and the mosquito stings a human being, how the parasite moves from the mosquito's belly up its thorax, and stinger, and transmits to a human via a mosquito bite. Til then, they thought malaria came from humid air.

"Walter Reed, anyone?"

A hand shot up. "Walter Reed Army hospital," a crew cut blond student replied crisply.

"Very good," Dr. Pike replied. "Tell us more."

"Not sure, sir, to be honest. Found a cure for yellow fever maybe?"

"You got it."

"I'm a veteran, sir. Did a tour of duty in Iraq."

"Well, God bless you. Thank you for your service. Yes, Walter Reed discovered a vaccine for the scourge of yellow fever, doing research in Cuba. Could have been a fancy doctor, anywhere he chose, Harvard grad, their youngest graduate ever. Instead, chose rugged, disease-infested yellow fever country, to help the soldiers stationed there, dropping like flies. Face turns yellow, swollen balloon, runaway fever. Quite a few of his assistants died from their experiments. That was roughing it. Confirmed the theory that yellow fever is transmitted by a particular mosquito species, rather than by direct contact.

"On his return to the States, he was hailed a hero. He died a year later from an amoebic infection contracted in Cuba.

"One more, then we'll call it a day. Alexander Fleming?"

A few hands were raised. "Yes," Dr. Pike called on a female student.

"Penicillin," she declared triumphantly.

"Good. How did he do it? Anyone know more?"

Silence. "Not exactly Michael Jackson on the fame-o-meter, is he?"

A few guffaws.

"During World War I, Fleming served in the Royal Army Medical Corps. He worked as a bacteriologist, studying wound infections in a makeshift lab in France. Through his research there, Fleming discovered that antiseptics commonly used at the time were ineffective or worse, due to their diminishing effects on the body's immunity agents. More soldiers were dying from antiseptic treatment than from the infections they were trying to destroy. Fleming recommended that, for more effective healing, wounds simply be kept dry and clean. His recommendations went largely unheeded.

"In September 1928, Fleming returned to his laboratory after a month away with his family, and noticed that a culture of Staphylococcus he had left out had become contaminated with a mold, later identified as Penicillium. He also discovered that the colonies of staphylococci surrounding this mold had been destroyed.

"Sheer serendipity? Not really. Fleming's expertise recognized what serendipity revealed to him.

"Later, he remarked, 'when I woke up just after dawn on September 28, 1928, I certainly didn't plan to revolutionize all medicine by discovering the world's first antibiotic, or bacteria killer. But I suppose that was exactly what I did.' First, he called the substance 'mold juice,' and then named it 'penicillin,' after the mold that produced it.

"Producing it in large batches, turns out to be another story, and took more than a decade. That for next time, perhaps. However, penicillin in mass quantities arrived in time to save thousands if not millions of veterans with wounds, fighting in WW2. And the rest, as they say, is history."

"Alright. You can go now," Dr Pike said, with a

fond wave, and sent them scurrying to their next class. "Medicine rocks," he called after them, then chastised himself, "a bit overly familiar perhaps, or preening."

Kimberly came up off to his side, and behind him. "Hi Dad," she said quietly.

"Take me to church," said R.

"You're joking," said Kimberly.

"Maybe, maybe not. People I admire found something important there. Solace, comfort, redemption even. Good conversation anyway. Exploring multiple dimensions, beyond our ken? Emily Dickinson made important connections there, psychic connections. W.H. Auden sang in the church choir in his later years. Joseph Conrad, author of *Heart of Darkness*, a man who explored, went to sea, and also his subconscious said, "there are excesses but it ennobles."

"A psychic connection, like Dionne Warwick and the Psychic Hotline?"

Kimberly teased playfully.

"No," said R. "I'm seriously looking for the lost chord, Kimberly. I'm not fooling around here."

"Did you ever hear the expression 'Zounds'?" said R.

"Like 'wow, amazing,' isn't it?," replied Kimberly.

"'Gods' wounds', from Elizabethean English. Shakespeare employed the term frequently in *Romeo and Juliet*, if I recall. Young lovers doomed by their family feuds. Also, in the afterword to *The Tempest*, Shakespeare called on Christian comforts to close the magic show. Milton posed the interesting question, is it better to be independent and rebellious and damned, or pious, and in the herd? But offered no way back from the youthful, rebellious excitements. Dante—ah, Dante—the human passage from inferno to purgatorio to paradisio. A great imaginative feat, a fest, an unfathomable heart song."

"I don't know," said Kimberly.

"I don't know," said R.

He crossed the room to where she stood and regarded her tenderly. "Am I crazy?" R. said.

"Silly," said Kimberly. "We'll go to church if you want. My parents go fairly often. Want to go this Sunday with them? I'll call them."

"Yes," said R. "I need a way. A way to break on through to the other side. Or the possibility of a way, anyway."

"Yes," said Kimberly.

"No."

"No."

"Yes."

"Yes/No/No/Yes, we were riffing on faith and doubt," declared R. warmly. "That's what I'm talking about," he said. "It's like new dimensions. We are like dogs in front of a tv set. Would we even recognize the supernatural narrative? Mother Theresa had doubts, she confessed."

"I heard my father lecture today," said Kimberly. "He said something that stuck in my mind."

"What?" said R., curious.

"'It's not our world.' He was talking about the history of medicine, made an offhand remark when a student asked why disease exists at all."

"Yes," said R. "It's not our world. It cuts both ways."

R.'s modest two bedroom apartment was 20 feet off the ground, in mid-air. R.'s ex-roommate, who had given up his lease, now in Florida permanently with his girlfriend (wedding bells in their near future apparently), described the $2 million renovation recently done, when R. moved in.

"The powers-that-be in the complex replaced pleasing wooden terraces with black metal railings and a stone-slab terrace floor. The terraces are stronger now, however the railings remind me a bit of the county jail," joked his roommate. "Such are the mysterious ways of progress."

But to R. the terrace was a blessing, and helped invest the humble abode with a patina of charm.

Each day R. would put out peanut bits, or suet, or bread crumbs, scatter this on the railing and on the terrace floor. So the birds came and would continue to come. A copse of trees about 15 feet from the terrace railing rustled and swayed in the breeze. R. could make out a nest, from his vantage on a comfy seat on the terrace. Also, a second nest, further out, in the copse of trees, to his right, barely visible. Oh, they would take their time, slowly at first. After awhile, they got to know R., apparently got accustomed to seeing him out there sitting, meditating, or reading, and would fly up and perch on the railing for tasty morsels, or peck on the terrace floor, a dozen feet or so from his legs.

"Tell me about the birds," said Kimberly.

"The birds, the birds," R. declared enthusiastically. "Robins come, sparrows, chocolate-y wrens, with blue markings on their neck, thrushes, and warblers mostly.

The warblers sing so prettily. They usually come one by one. Every so often, a pair will come, mates I suppose. A mother and her fledgling once, maybe, could tell by their disparate size, two sparrows."

The apartment complex was situated off a broad street, with large trees spaciously placed, down a long, winding driveway.

Kimberly arrived at R.'s apartment complex to check it out.

The humble two bedroom apartment boasted a nice, little skylite in the kitchen, a carpeted living room, and two bedrooms, a large mirrored closet space in each bedroom, and a walk in closet in the entry hall. Enough closet space for two, noted Kimberly.

They would not be fighting over closet space.

Over a period of months, Kimberly's clothes seemed to accumulate magically, nearly filling a large second closet, and pouring out onto the bed in the spare room.

R.'s desktop computer in the bedroom, and a laptop in the livingroom, competed with his Bose sound system, for his attentions.

"This is my mission control," R. declared one afternoon, not soon after his substitute teaching gig began. He had lucked into a two week stint, replacing a teacher on sick leave, and would need to bring home homework assignments, and papers to grade. They ate breakfast in the kitchen alcove, under the skylite, a pleasing touch. In the living room, R. kept a large mahogany cocktail table, with a marble slab in the middle, that he had scarfed from a garage sale long ago, and rebuilt and refinished, til it shined like new.

"Well, I would consider covering it with a clothe, so the wood doesn't pick up the pen strokes," said Kimberly practically.

"Well, I intend to grade the papers on the marble scrupulously," said R. "However, you're right, it can't hurt," said R. cheerfully.

"Look, the birds," R. exclaimed.

A sparrow was walking and pecking out on the terrace, nibbling the peanuts. "So tiny but they fly thousands of miles per year," said R. "Oh, to have wings like them."

"They fly and sing," said Kimberly. "They may be our closest relatives," she said presciently, if absurdly, knowing full well that according to the experts, and common knowledge, monkeys are our closest evolutionary relatives.

"Maybe," agreed R. enthusiastically. "Maybe."

"Let me read you a student paper I received today," said R. "This is from Alicia. We're studying the *Call of the Wild*, by Jack London."

"Okay," said Kimberly.

"Here's the assignment. Describe Buck's masters, in terms of their personalities and management abilities. Be specific."

Alicia's answer. "Judge Miller was Buck's first master. Their relationship was based on friendship. Judge Miller provided Buck with a luxurious environment and a relaxed, enjoyable life. Buck spent a lot of time with the judge's sons and daughters. Buck was his companion, his friend at home, his pet.

"After Buck was stolen, his master, the man in the red sweater, was a brutal man who let Buck know that he was the boss. Buck learned that if he did not obey, he would be beaten with the club. The man in the red sweater was in control over Buck and the law-giver.

"Perrault and Francois were English-French Canadian men, who needed Buck to deliver the express mail. Being with these men, Buck learned that life was not as easy as before and also learned how to manoever the sled. Perrault and Francois fed Buck an adequate amount of food and treated Buck fairly. Buck would only be punished if he deserved it. He would not be beaten for no reason. These two masters needed Buck for one thing and that was to deliver the express mail. They got the job done and no longer needed Buck. There was no close personal relationship between Buck and these masters.

"Hal, Charles, and Mercedes were the most disorganized and inexperienced of all the masters. They were "slobs" and didn't know how to pack their belongings or put a tent up. They also didn't know the first thing about taking care of dogs. They traveled with 14 dogs thinking they were traveling in style, not realizing how much food it takes to feed that many mouths. Charles and Hal treated Buck cruelly and unfairly. When the dogs were too tired to travel, they assumed they were hungry and kept feeding them. Mercedes, Hal, and Charles quarreled constantly and their journey was delayed because they did not let the dogs rest. Hal was going to kill Buck one day because he was too tired and had an uneasy feeling about traveling on thin ice.

Mercedes, Hal, and Charles drowned because of their stupidity and ignorance.

"John Thorton saved Buck's life by standing up to Hal and threatening his life if he struck Buck again. When he saw how brutally beaten Buck was, he pitied the poor Buck and could no longer see him get beaten. Thorton was kind and affectionate towards Buck. He was Buck's ideal master and Buck experienced genuine, passionate love for the first time. Buck never felt this way before in his life, not even at Judge Miller's place."

Out of what experiences does the Thornton-Buck relationship grow?

"Buck's first sign of loyalty towards Thorton happened at Circle City. A man named Burton struck Thorton and the next thing you knew, Buck viciously attacked Burton, tearing his throat open. Buck also saved Thorton's life when he fell into the violent, roaring rapids. The most amazing thing Buck did for Thorton was win a bet of 1,600 dollars in five minutes. Buck was to pull 1,000 pounds for 100 yards. Buck wanted to do this for Thorton because he felt that in some way he must do a great thing for John. Thorton inspired and encouraged Buck the whole time. It was out of love that they won this difficult task."

"Really good," said Kimberly.

"Isn't it?" said R. Was she being honest? He did not want her blowing smoke up his behind.

"Out of what experiences does the Kimberly—R. relationship grow?" teased Kimberly, when R. was done reading.

R. hesitated. Did she want a serious answer? "Kimberly saved R. from a car wreck, and nursed him to health, much like Thornton nursed the injured Buck," R. replied, with a straight face. After all, it was true.

Kimberly's eyes became misty.

"Play 'Misty' for me," R. joked, hoping to diffuse the tension. "You know, there's a Chinese proverb that says, 'once you save a person's life, you are responsible for that person, and have a duty to them.'"

"Confucius says"," Kimberly said nonchalantly. "We're American, not Asian."

The moment passed. She was being hardheaded.

"Well, the Asians have an ancient, venerable culture," R. stuttered. Now he got misty-eyed.

"I know," said Kimberly, closing the distance between them, with a big hug. "I'm so glad your teaching is going well. You will be an excellent teacher, I know it."

They sat on the sofa and kissed. Outside, the twilight bled over the wintry lawns, a backdrop for the couple in each other's arms, and the warm, cozy moment that fortifies and strengthens a youth with wounds that may heal, passing understanding, and scars that will remain, and strengthens what remains.

Later that week, R. asked Kimberly if she would play the audience, for a reading.

"Anything but infections," begged Kimberly, exhausted from a day of nursing classes.

My Most Embarrassing Moment—The April Fool of a Cosmic Jest.

"'Wait!'" I cried. "Please don't run; I've never kissed an African-American before.

"I ran after them as fast as I could until they slipped into a smoke-filled, alcohol-stenched house that happened to belong to my best friend. We had decided to throw the party the day before when Natalie's mother casually mentioned that she would be going to Monterey for the weekend with her boyfriend. Why not?, we had reasoned. It would only be a few friends over to share a couple of beers. Standing in the doorway, gazing drunkenly at the crowd, I realized that none of these people were my friends. In fact, I knew not one of them!

"I made my way to the back of the house, and into the bathroom. All the alcohol had hit my empty stomach, and I was suffering from an extremely severe, and unpleasant case of diarrhea. Realizing that Natalie had run out of toilet paper, I pulled a stiff, mildewed washcloth out of the hamper. After I had taken care of my business, I pulled up my pants, and exited the bathroom, not even thinking to flush the toilet or turn out the light. I was too out-of-it to even care.

"I walked down the hall to Natalie's bedroom seeking a quiet place to relieve the throbbing that started in my head, but had now reached my bare feet. Who knew where my shoes were? Who even cared?

"After using all the energy I could muster, in an effort to open the door, the thought occurred to me that someone had shoved the bed in front of it. I heard suppressed moans from behind the door, I giggled, and walked into the TV room next door. There I found Robby Doleta's and Carolyn Cato's naked bodies wrapped around each other. I couldn't stop staring. I was intrigued by how close together they were, how they both seemed to struggle, yet stay very intent on reaching the same goal. I left the room at a slow, and deliberate pace, but with an incredible heartache that I knew was not an effect of my drinking. Gazing aimlessly at my surroundings, I decided that the master bedroom was my last hope for peace and quiet.

"Peeking cautiously around the door, I received a slap in the face like none other. There, on the floor, was Lisa Everly making out with Don Ferris, the world's most gorgeous guy. Everyone knew Lisa was a lousy degenerate. Feeling useless, and unwanted, I leaned against the wall. Before I understood what had happened, I had slid to the floor and was crying hysterically. Between sobs I was faintly aware of people laughing at me as if I were putting on a show or something. This was when everything went black.

"I woke to a ringing that took awhile for me to figure out was the telephone."

"Hello."

"Hello, Natalie?" I was about to protest but the heavily accented voice, once again, vibrated into my body. "This is your mother. I called to remind you that although the clock reads 5:30 a.m., it is actually 6:30 a.m. daylight savings time."

"'Thanks.' Click."

"I lay my head down again, then shot up, suddenly becoming very aware of the predicament I was in. I ran to Natalie's room, fumbling in the dark for the compact discs I had loaned her for her party. With no luck, I grabbed my bag, started down the hall, and came to a dead halt in front of the disaster area that had once been called a living room. I was filled with disgust for what I saw, but I HAD to get home.

"On the lawn I discovered some hippie girl picking up beer cans, and bottles. She kept muttering, 'Must recycle…must recycle…' I thought it strange, but paid little attention. I started home.

"By now I could see, and smell the first signs of morning. The cold air nipped at my feet, and I walked faster. I hoped my parents would still be asleep when I came in, but the thought quickly left my head. In their minds it was still 5:30 in the morning. A sly smile spread across my face. I had just gotten away with it again. Suddenly, another thought occurred to me. I looked at my watch. Yes, today was April Fools."

"This paper brings up stuff, old bad stuff," said R. "A heck of a good writer in the making there, wouldn't you say?"

"Tell me," said Kimberly. "Express."

"Express train, or express yourself?"

"Express yourself, naturally," said Kimberly coolly. "You've never talked about high school."

"Well, you know. Foster home to foster home. There are cliques and being the new kid in town, I felt like an outlier, a misfit, I'd say. Seemed natural enough, at the time."

"Goth hair style, stuff like that?" Kimberly inquired.

"Drink, drugs. Even guns," said R. "Hardcore."

"Really," replied Kimberly.

"Unfortunately," said R., "I was a troubled youth. Listened to metal music mostly. A savage, incoherent anger required dosing and dulling with alcohol. Uppers, downers, black beauties. My foster parents had no clue, at first. I would keep a flask of Johnny Walker in my trench coat. I'd go to school reeking of marijuana. Get sent to the principal's office, my second home. Detention, suspensions, the school psychologist, the whole nine yards."

"Did your grades suffer?"

"School came pretty easy to me. Got good grades. My first sexual experience with Janie. There were three of us, we drove to the reservoir, on a warm summer evening. We hiked through the woods, and came out by the reservoir wall. We hung out there a long time. Talked about karma, life and death. Jimmy dared me to walk across. I dared him back. We were drunk, the night air filled with jasmine and honeysuckle moss. A 50 foot wall or so, like walking a tightrope, maybe a foot wide. A fall would have been fatal. Janie begged us not to go. We both kept walking, slightly nauseated. Janie ran around, came running up to us, "You guys are crazy. You could have been killed." Jimmy went off for a moonlight swim. Janie and I made out by the car for awhile. Jimmy was keeping us waiting, we called and called, and got no reply, Janie pulled me into the back seat. A thousand stars in the sky, we smoked a j. in the back seat and began talking our clothes off. I don't remember. That night I lost my virginity."

"What happened to Jimmy?"

"He came staggering back, drunk as a skunk, in his

underpants. Said he couldn't remember where he laid his clothes, still soaking from his midnight swim.

"We drove back home in a daze, I tiptoed into my foster home around 5 a.m., sure I'd get caught, but I did not."

"Whoa," said Kimberly.

"My high school years are a blur," said R. "I was lucky to get out alive. Lucky I got to college. Knowledge, books. So many different worlds. The military, they put a little starch into me, I must say."

"Guess so," exclaimed Kimberly.

"Always there like scars, you rip up, and the old wounds are still there. Below the surface."

"No," said Kimberly, "not anymore."

"Well, I don't know. I'm expressing."

"You're a teacher now. You've been through it, your season in hell. You're an artist and musician, don't forget. Now you're ready to help others with what you've learned. Be a leader."

R. kissed her. "That's so sunshine, optimism, tomorrow, I love it," said R. with tears in his eyes.

"Do you think you could have jumped?" said Kimberly, unexpectedly.

"Wasn't thinking about it, letting it happen, more like it. If…"

"If," said Kimberly.

"If it was meant to be," said R. "Open. Like the lion in the movie intro saying 'not tonight buddy. But I'll be back.'"

Kimberly enjoyed listening to him read.

He was a scruffy looking guy with luxurious brown

hair, and big, soft eyes, a little starter-beard, and a velvety, sonorous voice.

He seemed, to her, to animate the surroundings with vitality, a wild card element, unpredictable and quirky.

"One day, I stole my foster father's gun. I walked into the woods. Took a couple of pills, found myself sitting by a quiet stream. No one there but me. Sunlight streaming through the branches. The brown trees surrounding me, gently swaying in the summer breeze. They seemed sentient like witnesses, in a ceremonial pomp. I sat there and played with the gun, pointing it at my heart. I played 'stay alive here, leave life here.' I put my finger on the trigger. It seemed so restful, so easeful, to go to sleep forever. Birds snapped me out of it. Their song seemed so joyous, burbling over me, saying 'stay awhile, life rocks.'"

"Richard, that's horrible," Kimberly exclaimed.

"I'm expressing," replied R. "Isn't that what you wanted? Is it too much for you?"

"No, I can handle it," Kimberly decided, snuggling up, putting her head on R.'s chest. "But it scares me so."

"There's a road to recovery," said R. "Every saint has a past, every sinner has a future."

"You're on the road to recovery," encouraged Kimberly emphatically. "Forward, march. You would never have met me," Kimberly reminded him.

She sensed his bold, poetic spirit, when he read and when they were intimate. His aura, his deeds. The touch of desperation in his kiss gave their love an edge. Kimberly felt he really needed her, and in her a reciprocal feeling arose, needing him to need her. "A poet-philosopher, a music man, from the source," Kimberly felt, "emerges to love me."

Next morning, Kimberly, fully dressed, warmed up next to his softly breathing body. "Keeps me on my tippy toes, wanting more," she said, quietly kissing R.'s sleeping head, scars and all, before leaving for her 9 a.m. class.

"A daisy chain of vics, turned on by Dr. Feelgood, or a basically good guy, providing medical care to a gang of rock'n roll rebels, strung out on dope, with health problems, take your pick," March opened the call, challenging R. to respond.

"Tell me," said R. "Not enough information."

"You're telling me. That's the bane of my profession. Your case is keeping me busy. Galveston, Texas, Roanoke, Virginia, Los Angeles, I'm on a U.S. tour of my own, following the members of this girl band, long disbanded, that Dr. Feelgood hooked up with, long ago. I feel like singing Willie Nelson,

on the road again, I'm so stressed from being
on the road again.

"First, there's Ginny. A barely-out-of-high-school vixen, thin, long streaky blonde hair, breasts high in her sweater, pouty mouth, mischievious mien, so I gather from her pictures. The band pictures are very revealing. With a potty mouth, according to her bandmates. But on stage, a wildcat, their lead singer. Sound familiar?"

"Should it?" exclaimed R.

"Second, there's Little Barbie. A tall, broad-shouldered girl with long, straight brown hair, and big brown eyes. Liked to party hardy according to all involved, including Barbie. She played badass bass, and sang back up."

"Third, there's Betty. A sturdy blond with a pony tail, muscular legs, looks like an escapee from a cheerleading squad, ready for a gymnastics coach to lend a hand. She played drums, and sang back up also."

"Lastly, there's Louise. A pretty, waiflike mien, reddish brown hair, sharp little chin, witchy, wild and crazy, in her rocker days. Plays lead guitar, until Ginny takes over, and Barbie drops out."

"E-x-c-u-s-e me for asking, but what does all this have to do with my case, and Dr. Fairchild?"

"Ha ha," said March. "Ginny Rose, you heard of her?"

"The rock'n roller with one big hit or something, ten years ago?"

"She's a successful touring rock star to this day. Started young. She's Ginny in this band."

"So?"

"I talked to her. She told me about Dr. Fairchild."

"What did she say?" exclaimed R., suddenly interested.

"What didn't she say," exclaimed March. "That's the problem with these damned cases. It's like that story Rashemon, there's multiple points of view. Viewpoints are like assholes, everybody's got one."

"Okay, March. Did she have good things to say about him?"

"Well, basically Ginny's take is the girl band was getting gigs, playing places like Whiskey A Go Go, in

Austin, and building a buzz. You know, sex, drugs and rock'n roll. They went through guys like white on rice. It was getting out of hand, unruly fans, predatory characters hanging out after the show, enticing them with drugs. There were a rash of ODs at the time, from off-the-street dealers, and the girls got scared. They hooked up with Dr. Fairchild. He supplied them with Quaaludes mostly, and Percocet. He enjoyed being part of the rock'n roll scene, and they liked having him around. He was dependable, and became their protector, in a way. That's Ginny's take, anyway. It's been two decades since she's seen him, but she remembers him well. Says he was a bit of a party animal, and did become involved with a couple of band members, at the time, but was much preferred to the riff raff that hung around, looking for an easy score."

"Hmm," said R. "Maybe not so bad. What about the other girls?"

"According to Barb, reading from my notes, a young, struggling rock band looking for access to easy drugs, especially Quaaludes, finds a Dr. Feelgood, and invites him to a few shows, on the house. 'I do something for you, you do something for me. I scratch your book, you scratch my back' kinda thing. Barb remembers him as a sleazy guy. Always talking up, and flattering them, and their music, in a calculating way. She's not a fan, calls him Dr. Feelgood. Had a bad feeling about him from the start."

What else?" said R.

"Well, Betty's take is between Ginny and Barb, I'd say. Dr. Fairchild starts out like a father, or older brother figure, chaperones them around, protects them from more obvious predators, insinuates himself into their circle with his prescriptions and doctor aura, and non-judgemental attitudes. He gets to relax with a bunch of pretty girls who like to "get down," goes to their wild and crazy parties. Witnesses, and participates apparently, in stuff going down, sex and drugs. Starts an intense affair with Louise, the lead guitar player. That's where the gals all agree. That did not sit well with any of them."

"Louise ended up sliding into a serious drug dependency, so she could not perform with the band. The band felt they had no choice but to let her go, after her showing up shitfaced and falling down all over the place, drunk and on quaaludes one too many times.

"They called Dr. Fairchild numerous times, and begged him to help her.

"He'd come and scrape her off the floor, and drive her home. A couple of years later, she was dead."

"Whoa. Dead. She was just a kid. What from?"

"Drug overdose, apparently."

R. whistled loudly. "Does not pass the smell test."

"Well, you could say that. But stuff happens. She was a crackhead, at the end, they say. Heartbroken she'd been fired from the band. 'Dr. Fairchild did his best,' according to Ginny, reading from my notes. In fact, got her into a fancy, reputable rehab facility, and paid the bill himself. It didn't matter, she ran away."

"Damn," said R.

"Bohemian Rhapsody", "Space Oddity", "Spiders From Mars," were three of Louise's favorite songs, and Queen, David Bowie and Slash, among her influences.

Ginny and Louise wrote most of the band's songs. Louise was good on the lyric side, according to them all. After she died, it cut the heart out of the band, they broke up soon after.

"Only Ginny pushed on, making a career in music. Barb became a real estate agent. She's married with three kids. Betty's a paralegal in L.A. Works for an entertainment lawyer, keeps her hand in the music biz, anyway. She married a broker, who likes rock 'n roll, she has a couple of kids in college already."

"Lift every voice, share the dream, bury the chain," exclaimed R.

"Huh?" said March.

"Tell me more about Louise," said R.

"Let's see, looking at my notes," muttered March. "Pretty waif. Wore black, black stretch pants, black sweaters, made quite an impression with her long hair, rolling past her shoulders, I've seen the photographs, she was a looker. By the way, one more thing."

What's that?" replied R.

"Louise gave birth to a son, before she died."

"What happened to him?"

"That's where the trail goes cold," said March dramatically. "Given up for adoption, apparently. According to her mother, who I talked with briefly on the phone, not in person. We're on your dime kid, I make judgement calls, no pun intended."

"Who was the father?" inquired R.

"Dunno," responded March. "Are you thinking what I'm thinking?"

"Maybe..."

"Maybe. Dr. Feelgood's in a jam, if his rock'nroll girlfriend gets pregnant?"

There was dead silence on the phone.

"You know how it is, sex, drugs, rock'n roll. Stuff happens. But that was a long time ago, and in another state, and besides the wench is dead," March remarked elaborately.

"Shakespeare," said R. "*Othello.*"

"I don't know," said March. "I'm only saying..."

"Well," said R. He paused dramatically. "The wench may be dead, but we're not. I'd like to find out more about her."

"Kid, what more could we do? Where's this leading?" March wondered plaintively. "Take a step back. Look at the big picture."

"Okay," said R. "Dr. Feelgood knocks up our rock'n roller, and freaks out when she tells him she's pregnant, and decides to get rid of her. Gives her bad drugs, on purpose. Or treats her maliciously, cuts off her stash, so she goes running to a random street corner, and ODs."

"Sheer speculation," said March. "Would make for a middlin' TV movie at best. But in real life. Doubtful. Doctors tend to be careful about stuff like procreation. Plus, the girl had a rep as bein' wild and crazy and into drugs, prior to pal-ing around with Dr. Fairchild. Indeed, sounds like he may have been a moderating influence on her, for a couple of years anyway."

"Well, it's a long and winding road," said R. "Bumpy too. With many detours. A boulder could roll down from the hills, and crush any one of us. I feel a connection with this gal, God knows why. What will happen to us all in 50 years?"

"We'll be gone," chuckled March. "My daughter will be a grandmother, hopefully."

"On that note. Keep digging…" R. declared.

"How shall we leave this then?"

"Up in the air. 'The game's afoot,' Sherlock Holmes would say."

"I could go see her mother," offered March.

"The case of the dog that didn't bark," remarked R. wisely.

"Now I'm completely befuddled," admitted March. "What dog? Reminds me how I felt when my daughter announced in the school paper that she was a lesbian. Utterly perplexed, not the half of it. Each day I wake up and wonder what new surprise, delight, havoc, or confusion my daughter will unleash on my wife and I. She's a bit of a wild child, I'm afraid. Gives us an opportunity to have a face to face, every so often, and in the middle of my lecture I realize I cannot stop what I started, and all the while my daughter smiles like the cat that swallowed the canary."

"The cat that swallowed the canary. That's funny," replied R.

"It's spooky," March retorted. "I enjoy rock'n roll, but I'd have a heart attack if my daughter joined a rock'n roll band. Like the Stevie Wonder song, or whoever sang it, 'Spooky.'"

"Good luck with that, March. Bewilderment. The posture of an amazed witness. Go see her mother. Later March," said R. and folded his phone up.

R. turned to Kimberly with an odd, excited look on his face. “The game’s afoot,” he said.

11

After a few months convalescence, nursing bruised ribs, and torn sinews, and head wounds, R. found himself cultivating his external side on the road to recovery. R. in his used red Pontiac GT became a familiar sight around town. R. in his used red Pontiac GT buying strawberries and cantaloupe at the fruit stand at the side of route 65. R. in his used red Pontiac GT enjoying little league games, watching the kids play, the runners run, as late afternoon turns to dusk, for the sheer pleasure of it. R. in his used red Pontiac GT pulling up to the local fitness center, for a workout in the morning. R. in his used red Pontiac GT revving it up before parking and attending his education classes at UConn.

Mostly, R. felt rejuvenated, grateful to be alive. Though a little tentative about his future.

R.'s road to recovery became just that when he began substitute teaching. His present assignment, a half hour drive into rural Connecticut, provided a leisurely, windy half hour or so, through backroads, and rolling hills. He was surprised to note farms on his way, ponies standing in a pasture, or browsing by a fence. The fresh air and chilly autumn morning invigorated him, responding to the pleasure of the early morning drive.

After windy turns and curvaceous swings, R. received a bit of a thrill with a glimpse of the red brick school building, high on the hill. Yellow school busses roared by, while he stopped for a moment on the road shoulder. Education. Learning. Society. Knowledge transmission. The colors, the experience. Now he was becoming a part of it. He felt for a moment like the King of Cats. After months of weakness, disability, fear, insecurity, he emerged from his shell. More or less intact, physically anyway, he begins a task, and rejoins society, part of the great stream of commerce, education, civility, life. He drove up the hill in his used red Pontiac GT, feeling like an impostor, a spy in the house of kids and authority figures. But that was okay for now. Forward, march. He would have to ease into his transformation, one day at a time.

The yellow school busses formed a semi-circle, atop the hill, expelling their charges, vivid, vivacious, bright eyed, talking, screaming school kids, and gave him a kick.

He sauntered into the principal's office, amid their flying colors, to pick up his lesson plans for the day. "Prince of Cats reporting for duty," he said to Stacy, the pert blonde receptionist, secretary, behind the front desk. With mild eyes and mien, at her slightly alarmed glance, R. replied, "only joking, that's Shakespeare."

R.'s hand dug into the sick-day teacher's mailbox, and withdrew the lesson plans for the day. R. would have a half hour or so to prepare, during their homeroom period.

Each day was different, in terms of the lesson plan.

At quite a few schools, R. was on call, grades 7 to 12, for English or history.

But the kids' faces, they knocked him out, how lively, vivid, bright eyed, eager they were for action. They wanted to learn, most of them. Even if they did not know it, they wanted to learn. They wanted a happening day, a growing day, an opportunity to shine, maybe for a few moments be a star, be a participant in a happening flow, and learning and growing were a part of the flow, indeed the bubbly, the sparkle.

He found his way to the staff room, intending to look over the lesson plan for 1st Period. A little room with a microwave, and coffee maker, a table, a gnarly old sofa, and a few orange chairs. "Hi," he greeted the older lady sitting at the table, grading papers apparently. "Hello," she said peremptorily, intent on her task. "*Romeo and Juliet*, the class has already read it, choose a few discussion points, either mine below, or try your own," Ms. Paul, the missing-in-action teacher instructed him. R. could live with that. He knew the play well, from college days.

"Who are you?" the lady inquired suddenly.

"Subbing for Ms. Paul today," R. replied cheerily. "Looks like *Romeo and Juliet* for first period, I'm comfortable with that. Love the bard," said R. smoothly. "Also sub in history, if you ever need one," R., continued.

She looked at him over her reading glasses. "I'm Ms. Euler," she said frostily. "I teach high school history. Any sub of mine would really have to know his stuff. Let me give you a little quiz?" she said, with a touch of disdain.

"Go for it," smiled R.

"Who was our 21st president?"

"That would be Chester A. Arthur," R. replied swiftly.

"Alright," she said. "That was an easy one. Who received the most votes in 1876?"

"Samuel Tilden did, if you are speaking of popular votes. However, that's a bit of a trick question. Although the democrat from New York, Tilden won the popular vote, Rutherford B. Hayes won the electoral vote, and became our 19th president. Only time in American history where the candidate who won the popular vote, did not become president."

"Very good," she said, if a bit reluctantly.

"Here's my card, with my contact info," R. replied smoothly, handing her a card. She read, "Richard Rodgers/ tutors English, American history/also teaches piano and guitar. Call #####, or contact #####."

R. glanced at the play, refreshing his memory, then it was off to 1st period.

Entering an empty classroom, the waiting seats, the old blackboard, the chalky smell, brought back memories, it was magical. He wrote his name in large, straight letters on the blackboard. One by one the crowd shuffled in, and took their seats. "Oh, a sub," one groaned.

"Hello, I'm Mr. Rogers. A pleasure to meet all of you. I will be substituting for Ms. Paul today. Let's do attendance." R. called out a name, and a student replied. A couple were absent. "Peggy's in Florida, for her grandfather's funeral," a student offered, explaining a non-response.

"Alright, let's get to it," said R. "You guys have read *Romeo and Juliet,* according to Ms. Paul. Spent quite a lot of time on it. Any general impressions?"

Three or four hands shot up. R. looked out at the

class. Mostly caucasian, a few latino, a few asian, a few frican americans. "Yes," said R. to a burly guy with thick black hair, and a swarthy complexion.

"A couple of losers who couldn't handle the pressure, and offed themselves before they gave themselves a chance to live."

"Hmm," said R. "There's a point of view, with substance. Wouldn't call them losers though, maybe confused would be more like it."

"Anyone?"

"Victims of love, due to their stupid, ignorant parents, who did not seem to care, and the gang fighting all around them that sucked them in."

"Yes," said R. "The parents seem rather isolated from their children's experiences, throughout the play, repeating the same old platitudes, talking down rather than talking to, their children. But that doesn't mean they didn't love them just that they were out of touch. Good."

"Anyone else?" inquired R.

"Why do we have to read this? It's not even the same language," a husky guy towards the back, complained.

"Hmm," said R. "Well. Anyone respond?"

A girl in the second row came to the rescue. "This is a beautiful story. Two young lovers against the world. I totally relate. The world can be a very ugly place," she said emphatically.

"How do you relate?" inquired R. gently.

"Well, this is personal but…I have a boy friend and my parents do not like him, and say I cannot see him anymore. They are driving me crazy."

"Keep the dialogue with our parents going," R.

encouraged. "Maybe it will work out in time, one way or the other. But do know, they care about you, and want the best for you, though they may not excel at expressing that," R. offered. He did not know really what to say.

"There's gang warfare in rap songs. Here in Connecticut, the Bloods, Latin Kings, and R-2 Crips are fighting. Like in *Romeo and Juliet,"* an African American kid offered.

"There's violence, oppression, and gangs out there in the real world, it's true," said R. "Though I would urge you to steer clear of that. Shakespeare's depiction in *Romeo and Juliet,* relating to family feuds and gangs, have their corollary today, in certain parts of the country. Young lovers have eyes for each other, it's a new beginning. The world intrudes, breaks in, doesn't matter if you say "thou" or "you," "hath" or "has", the same forces are in play. Hopefully, we're making progress here and there," concluded R. , in a slightly joking tone.

"Yeah, we have machine guns, and Uzis now," a kid towards the back joked in kind.

"We have the United Nations, in politics, we have nuclear disarmament, we have therapists, we have counselors, it's better now," a girl in the front row exclaimed dramatically.

R. clapped his hands, saying "well, really neat discussion."

"What do you guys make of Friar Laurence? What was his role in the play? Do you think he was good or evil?"

"The friar was definitely good," said a girl with black hair, and black eyeshadow, and tattoos. "He was the only adult who was concerned, and cared about them, really. He tried to warn them, how opposites can combine and be explosive, and create destruction, if not carefully controlled. Like gasoline and fire. Each by itself is helpful and beneficial, but when you combine them you have a fire."

"Very good," said R. "Excellent point."

"If not for the friar, Romeo and Juliet would never have committed suicide," a kid in the back, with tats, sneered. "It was the friar who instructed Romeo to purchase the poison from a dealer, and look how that turned out."

"Not quite," said R., encouragingly. "The friar marries Romeo and Juliet in an attempt to stop the family feud. He offers Juliet a fake poison, to save her from her family's intentions, an enforced marriage to Paris the next day."

"The friar means well, and devises a plan in good faith. He understands the power and sincerity of their young love. But the Friar's confused. And the plan goes wrong," counters the girl with black hair and black eyeshadow. "And all hell breaks loose."

"No good deed goes unpunished," quipped a blonde, with long hair, in the third row.

The bell rang, and they picked up their books and started to leave.

"Good discussion," sang R. after them. "Good discussion," one or two turned back and replied.

Onto Period 2.

After a hard, busy, but successful day substitute teaching, driving home from school, meager though it was, having accomplished the lesson plan, gotten the students involved in a few discussions, R. felt like he was on his road to recovery.

How could he ever repay Kimberly?

Well he understood there is a darkness that comes between, darkness in the world, darkness in the mind and heart, not to mention moods, ebbs and flows. But they crossed a river together, they were on a journey together, and that experience was formative, and integral. Way down R. resolved to value that, honor that, hold that dear. Given there was a sacred and profane, each held within the power to turn the key, transform, morph, improve their situation with a positive attitude. A cliché but also true. Like turning on the ignition of his car. Kimberly and he, that was reality. A sacred bond, like Romeo and Juliet. Like Seigfried and Roy. Like Mutt and Jeff. "A comedy routine is in the air," R. said aloud to his windshield.

From feeling maimed and feeble, to participate in this societal adventure, felt like a privilege.

"You've come a long way, baby," R. murmured, no cynicism on the horizon.

Still, all in all, a substitute teacher, a day in the life. Even though he had gone from a two week stint where he was in charge of the classroom, and gave assignments, back to a day-to-day "on call", that was alright. He was gaining experience, the students liked him. Admin seemed satisfied.

R. turned on his radio, and heard the biblical tones of CCR, "better run through the jungle, don't look back."

"Rainwater, a supplement that rain made more of..."

R. awoke muttering, from a dream. Kimberly departed for a class, and he fell asleep again, not receiving a school assignment call for the day, only to awaken to his cellphone ringing.

"9 a.m.," realized R., juggling his phone.

The phone ring was "Miracles" by Jefferson Airplane.

"If only you believe in miracles like I believe, we'd get by," a pretty melody anyway.

"Richard, March here," a cheery voice on the other end boomed. "I've made reservations to fly out to Colorado, and visit Louise's mother, she says she'll talk to me about Louise. Seems like Louise's room with her things, from childhood, anyway, is being kept up by her mom."

"Swell," R. replied, a bit sleepily. "A daisy chain of vics, like you said."

"Let's hold our horses," March replied. "Clearly you can't stand the guy, however, in balance, all in all, like I explained, there are shades of gray, based on what we're hearing from the witnesses. Let's not be a wicked jury and figuratively hang a guy before we hear the facts."

"Right you are," said R. "Haven't had my coffee yet," explained R., tumbling out of bed, and stumbling towards the kitchen. "Kimberly tells me the same thing."

"Gotcha," March laughed, in a friendly way. "Well, you were the one who coined the phrase about him," shot back R., a trifle annoyed now.

"Ho ho ho," joked March. "That's private eye lingo. Got to parse the evidence and evaluate all possible scenarios. Comes with the territory. We dream of the big score, you know."

"Shades of gray," said R., thoughtfully, savoring his coffee. "Hey, are you related to Mike Nesmith, in the Monkees? You know, the band from the 60s?"

"You got me," March replied. "A distant relation. A few years ago, I got on the 'puter and went to a site familytree.com or some such site. Have a relative who got bayoneted in the civil war. Have a relative who was in the navy in the War of 1812. Way back there. Also, found Mike Nesmith, from the Monkees, way off on the left, a second or third cousin, if I recall."

March sang boisterously on the phone.

Hey hey we're the monkeys,
and people say we monkey around,
but we're too busy singing,
to put anybody down.

"We're the monkeys," agreed R.

"Richard, do have a coincidence for you."

"A coincidence"?, R. responded.

"Yes, my daughter turned me on to this, by the way. I spread out your case files on the table, here in the dining room. I work here often, while my wife and daughter watch tv, or my daughter does her homework, or whatever. The other evening my daughter popped by with her snack in hand, and noted out of the blue, 'the same birthday.'

"I didn't understand what she was referring to, brushed it off. I've got my head in these stacks of reports from the Connecticut State Board of Health. Looking for patterns there."

"Oh, I found one the other day," R. interrupted enthusiastically. He added a little milk to his half-consumed cup of coffee, getting up to speed. "A complaint against the doctor. On the internet."

"Tell me," said March, all ears.

--"Concerned neck fusion surgery. The patient was yelping on a site, forget the name at the moment, in my notes, not Yelp but another one designed for stuff like this, alerts to the public. Really down on Dr. Fairchild. Said the doctor was negligent, with reckless disregard. Said the doctor performed this surgery on him and told him the surgery was successful. Instructed him to take it easy, you know, wear a neck brace, get into rehab. However, the patient's neck did not improve, in fact, felt worse, so he went to get a second opinion. The second specialist (orthopedist), explained the surgery was a failure. The neck bone did not fuse. Said the patient's severe pain, and restricted movement was due to a botched surgery, or implied that anyway."

"What else?" said March.

"That's his M.O., he lies and covers up," R. said heatedly.

"And," said March.

"Well," said R. "there were a couple of responses from prior patients of Dr. Fairchild. There's an opportunity for response, of course. They leaped to Dr. Fairchild's defense. The first mentioned how successful his neck fusion surgery was. The second mentioned that his neck fusion was successful also, and stressed the importance of following to the letter the doctor's post-operative instructions. Went on and on about how a fused neck may become un-fused, post op, if the neck moves, due to even a relatively minor jolt, say in a car. Also, went on to say that the success of the operation takes months to determine. Implied the patient's condition was due to his own post-op negligence, or bad luck, or whatever. Very strenuously defended Dr. Fairchild, said experts had told him his was a difficult case, to be aware, said he'd had an excellent experience with Dr. Fairchild, 100% recovered, and would be forever grateful to him."

"So, there you go," said March. "I'm finding the Connecticut State Board of Health complaints are similar, to a degree. They consist of bad results, disappointing results in complex, high-risk surgeries. You feel for the patients, of course. God, these are life-altering surgeries after all. There are patients who will either walk or be confined to a wheelchair. Patients who will either be maimed for life, or be reborn to lead a normal existence, so called. Very high hurdles, medically. He takes on patients who other doctors turn down, who would not dare to perform the surgery. He's called a "hero" and a "savior" by many of his patients. All in all, the Connecticut State Board of Health gives him a pass on every complaint filed. They hand it off to a panel of experts. The panel makes an evaluation, and completes a report. Of course, the decision takes about four years from the time of the complaint, to be closed, and made available to the public, under the Freedom of Information Act. Of course, thousands of procedures. Many complaints, around 155 complaints, have occurred in the last four years and are pending, a huge cluster of complaints."

"Yes, but didn't you say the State Board of Health

there suffers from a 'rubber stamp' reputation, and will tend to support the doctors?"

"True," said March. "Their reputation is lousy. Partly due to lack of funding, and staffing, and the wait-times involved. The State Board ranks in the bottom 10% of State Boards of Health across the country, based on their outrageous wait-times and their procedural loopholes. But only a few law suits against Dr. Fairchild apparently.."

"Perhaps he settled them, with a confidentiality agreement," R. hypothesized.

"Perhaps. He's a smooth operator, no matter how you cut it," said March. "Hey, look at you. You got your second opinion. Your doctor, who was he?"

"Dr. Kranaidas."

"Dr. Kranaidas gave you an unbiased second opinion, and explained you got a good result, and Dr. Fairchild did a competent job, in an emergency situation."

--"Yes, but I smelled alcohol on his breath. He called me a 'deadhead' while examining my head," R. reiterated heatedly.

"Richard, I understand," March said warmly. "I empathize. If a doctor behaved that way with me, I'd be concerned also. Or a member of my family, I'd be hitting the roof. There's certainly enough here to raise concerns, no doubt about it, the frequency of complaints, the nurse's affidavit, testifying that she witnessed Dr. Fairchild drinking on the job. You may well be doing everyone who comes into contact with him professionally a public service."

"I'll let it go when I'm ready to, in time, I suppose," said R. "If there's no smoking gun. But it warrants a look, right?"

"Right you are," said March. "By the way, do you believe in coincidences?"

"Depends," said R. "Coincidences, ah."

R. heard a click on the line. "Richard, got an emergency," March explained. "Talk later."

Kimberly was busy cooking chicken, with potatoes, and broccoli. R. was sitting out on the terrace in his jacket, though it was 45 degrees there. He liked the cold weather, probably made newly bearable due to Kimberly. The sun rose and set with her, in R.'s world view.

"Richard, March here again. How are you?"

"Alright, March. What happened? A wronged spouse finally pull the trigger on her cheating mate? Or a shady Craig's List escort service gal meet her end at the hands of the local psycho?"

"Last year, with a case like that, I'm afraid. Stuff happens. How's Kimberly?"

"She's right here," R. replied. "Sends her regards. I'll tell you March, without her, I'd be a candidate for a bungee jump with no cord off the Medical Foundation balcony, you know, the one with the flower exhibit and balloons suspended from the ceiling. Splat, I'd be the miracle of the rose."

--"Stop talking nonsense," March exclaimed, abruptly. "I've got enough trauma for today. My daughter Jasmine was in a fender-bender. She only passed her drivers exam a week or two ago. Jesus!"

"Is she alright?" exclaimed R., alarmed.

"Thank God, yes. Shaken up, angry tears. But no injuries to speak of. By the way, the other guy's fault."

"Yikes, March, glad to hear she's alright," R. exclaimed warmly.

--"Right by her school, "March added. "You see, you and I were talking about your car accident and now my daughter's recovering from a car accident. What a coincidence. Or something more?"

--"There's a phenomena called quantum entanglement," said R. "You probably don't want to hear about it."

"Tell me," said March, the detective.

--"Oh, in theoretical physics, subatomic particles when they cross paths and collide, seem affected by the future behavior of the particles they collide with. Or rather, they seem continually influenced, if that makes sense."

"No, it doesn't," said March.

"There's a saying in theoretical physics 'the theory may be just crazy enough to be true.' No one really understand quantum physics, the experts are the first to confess. Anyway, we're in a macroscopic world, way too large for quantum entanglement."

"Glad to hear that," replied March. "I've collided with some pretty gnarly characters in my time. Ho ho ho."

"Me also," responded R. "A tough crowd back at the pinball factory, where I worked for a spell. The Army, well you know."

"Anyway, Richard. My daughter, I started to tell you. Oddly, are you sitting down?"

"Yes," said R. "What?"

"Your birthday, according to my intake form, is on May 18, 1990, right?"

"Yes," R. said. "That's right."

"Remember Louise, we talked about her?"

"Of course," exclaimed R.

"She gave away her son, put him up for adoption, remember?"

"Yes. So?"

"His birth certificate reads May 18, 1990."

--Dead silence. Pregnant silence.

--"That's a coincidence," said R., exhaling audibly.

After recovering his equilibrium and gathering his wits, R. remarked, "March, have you heard of synchronicity and Littlewood's Law of Miracles?"

"Can't say that I have," March admitted. "Maybe a Police song. Tell me."

"Well, synchronicity, a concept or theme, formulated by Karl Jung. Very interesting and entertaining idea. The structure of reality includes, in principal, an acausal connection which manifests in significant, meaningful coincidences."

"English, please," replied March.

"Jung used to it help explain the paranormal, for example. Also, Jung's archetypes, and the collective unconscious."

--"Don't get it. How?" exclaimed March.

--"Well, Jung felt he found a governing dynamic that underlies the whole of human experience, and extends into the realm of the emotional, psychological, and spiritual. You know, phenomena like ESP, the astral plane."

"Alright," said March. "Interesting. Tell me about Littlewood's Law of Miracles."

"Well," said R. thoughtfully. "I suppose one could view Littlewood's Law of Miracles the opposite side of the coin. A pragmatic approach to coincidences and so called "miracles." Littlewood, a professor of mathematics at Cambridge, if I recall, took a shot at demystifying "the miraculous" with an empirical approach. His basic thesis being that this scattering of rare "coincidences" or "miracles", comes with the territory in statistics, and fit under the extreme end of the bell curve, that's how I interpret it anyway.

"Littlewood defines a miracle as an exceptional event of 'special significance,' occurring at a frequency of one in a million. He assumes a person is alert and awake a certain number of hours a day, he assumes 8 hours a day, and in that time a person will see or hear about 1 event per second, exceptional or unexceptional. In 35 days or so, under these assumptions, do the math, a person will experience about 1 million sensory events. So once a month, the "strangest" will arouse in us that wonder, or discomfort, or awe, that causes us to label, depending on temperament and attitude, an event a "coincidence" or a "miracle."

"You don't say," said March, laughing. "How did you come by all these arcane notions?"

--"Oh, I'm a believer in multiple dimensions, far beyond the four dimensions commonly accepted. Imagine gold fish swimming in a garden pond. Their world is below the surface. Imagine a person inserting his hand into their world for a moment, and dropping a tasty treat. Manna from the sky, March. With multiple dimensions, the hand in the sky operating actions in our "fish pond," as it were, becomes not magic, but sufficiently advanced technology to flummox or shock us. It's kind of neat that every so often we seem to be called, or forced to realize the active presence of the heavens, in action in our world. The religious interpret this as "the hand of God." Others, perhaps, accept the mystery."

"Well, Richard, you surprise me, with all this advanced, theoretical stuff.

"I'll ask you, are you sitting down once more?"

"Yes," said R. The chances of sharing the same birthday as another person, was that 1 in 23? No, that was if you have a room full of 23 people, there's a 50% chance that two will share a birthday, R. recalled. Anyway, certainly was a coincidence.

"You're sure you're sitting," March exclaimed, cajolingly.

"I'm sitting on the sofa here. What?" exclaimed R.

"Good. Because this is a doozy, "replied March. "Louise' son's name, who she gave up for adoption, was Richard Rodgers."

You could have heard a mouse click.

"Kimberly," R. called. "I need you."

"What's up," Kimberly strode in, from the kitchen. "Talk to March," said R. "Deep water."

Surprised, amazed, astounded. The unforeseen contingency, the bolt from the blue, the wonder. The eye-opener deluxe, the thunderclap.

Surf's up, white horses, billows. Froth, spindrift, seaspray.

Kimberly put down the phone in shock, which however turned into a thoughtful look.

"A coincidence," she exhorted gently.

--"This will cause a revolution in my perspective," R. said in a bold, confused, vaguely threatening way.

"Richard," Kimberly said, going over to the sofa, and sitting beside him. "Want to watch TV? How about Survivors, Thailand?"

12

Ginny Rose. Female rock n' roll pioneer. The female David Bowie. Ginny enjoyed many write ups in the music magazines early in her career, even made a *Time Magazine* cover one year. But to her, it was not about being female. And the flattering comparison, yes, but she was her own person. That is why folks continued to come out and hear her music, while the years flew by, regardless she was in her 40s now.

The whole industry was undergoing a tectonic shift, with the internet advances, and streaming music, in particular. Youth loved music, needed music, and listened to music as intensely as before, since the Beatles anyway. However, the whole dynamic between star entertainer and their audience was changing. These days, most anyone could buy a computer and learn a software program or two, and build up a home studio, and aspire to make listenable, well produced music. Assuming they could play the instruments, and even then there were loops, beat shops, and auto-tune, to improve the groove. What's more, since Napster and the mp3 days, in the late 90s, folks wanted their music free, or nearly free. For a modest subscription fee each month sites like *Pandora* and

Spotify, gave them that option. Not to mention *Itunes*, and *youtube*, where video and music are free. Also, notable independent music sites, and individual musician web sites, were streaming music for free. Everyone wanted to be a star.

Ginny rose through the ranks, in the music biz. She built a following, concert by concert, tour by tour. Finally, a record company signed her. Her tough girl, edgy rock'n roll persona, with her arty wigs and tats, unique guitar riffs and style, found a paying audience. But it was tough times for old-school professional musicians. Her one radio hit was years ago. People were not buying CDs like they used to. Ginny enjoyed playing, but disliked touring, the grueling travel by plane, or by bus, from gig to gig. She was on a tight budget, with a hired band and a couple roadies. But she needed to do that now, in order to make a living.

When March Nesmith introduced himself, backstage in Tulsa, Oklahoma, amid the greasepaint, and the beer, and screaming and dancing, she could barely hear him. But when he mentioned Louise, she snapped out of it and focused.

Louise. She had not thought about Louise in awhile. Her heart beat strangely faster for a moment. She walked outside with March into a windy November night. Plumes of vapor filled the air, while they talked. Their silhouettes wavered on the cement wall of the auditorium where she'd just finished a concert.

"How goes the tour?" asked March. "We talked on the phone, remember?" March was saying. "You said you found Louise's journal."

"Grinding it out, you know," responded Ginny. "Music's an upper."

Ginny remembered the pre-glory days. Sweet Louise, a good bass player. Junkie Louise, they called her, near the end. She kept coming to rehearsals, stoned out of her mind, to all appearances, could barely stand up. Only later, when March called, did she find Louise's journal in her storage unit. She did not remember its contents at all, doubted that she ever read it really, could not remember receiving it in the mail. Maybe she was so down on Louise at the time, she threw it in a backroom and forgot about it. Louise's journal had laid in a box with assorted junk and memorabilia for 25 years.

"I read it for the first time a few days ago, after your call," Ginny recalled, with tears in her eyes. "Broke my heart, I'll tell you. I felt terrible. If only we had known."

"Known what?" inquired March.

"That she was pregnant. She never told us. Never breathed a word. Damn!"

Well…" March started.

"She was stubborn that way," Ginny recalled. "Probably did not want us feeling sorry for her. Or asking the inevitable questions, who's the father, what are you going to do? Do you think I'm a horrible person?" she turned to March suddenly.

"Are you?" said March.

"Here's her journal. I'm handing it off to you. You decide," Ginny declared. And she reached into her purse and drew out a purple, velvet-covered notebook-sized journal.

"Thank you," March exclaimed. "Louise speaks, in

this journal. Like I explained, I'm representing a client, we're investigating her doctor friend, Dr. Fairchild. Dr. Fairchild did surgery on my client, following a serious car accident. By the way, my client plays music, also. Richard's only 25. A brilliant musician, I've heard it said. You know what's the strangest part?"

"Huh?" said Ginny.

"Richard may be Louise's son. Shares the same name and birthday, anyway, brought up in foster homes."

"Whoa," exclaimed Ginny. "Blow my mind, Starman lives."

March clutched the notebook in hand. "I'm sorry," Ginny exclaimed.

Louise's Journal. 12-14-90. Turning into a valium-head. Up all night without them. Take three at a time just to get a few hours sleep. No mojo. No bueno.

My back is killing me.

Lugging the amps around night after night for years will do that to a girl's back.

Arthur Fairchild's been a good friend. He's referred me to specialists, he comes over to check on me.

In pain all the time. A ruptured disc they say. They recommend surgery. I'm scared of the knife. Say the surgery may make it worse.

12-25-90. Christmas day. Alone in my apartment. Ginny, and Betty and Barb are disgusted with me. I cannot play guitar like the band needs. I can barely stand. We're drifting apart, I can feel it.

They're so pissed off, they think I'm a loser, a pillhead. If they understood how my back hurts...

1-18-91. Sleeping into deep depression and extreme drug dependency. My craving for extreme sensation maybe. It's too unbearable, unless I'm high. Masks the horror anyway. I don't want to live in constant pain. I'm frightened to be crippled. Play guitar in a wheelchair? Get me out of here.

1-30-91. Kicked out of the band. Arthur wants me to go into rehab. I have to clean up, he says. It's nice of him to offer to pay the bill.

2-18-91. Back worse than ever. Everyone hates me. I'm a loser. Ran away from rehab. Need oblivion for awhile. Over and out.

2-24-91. Last Will and Testament. When I lay awake at night, the wolf is knocking on the door. Big, slavery jaws, come and get me already.

A last note to my son. I love you. I did not want to give you up. Your mother's a junkie. Not fit to be a mother, it's true. In another lifetime, my son. We will meet again. I will hold you in my arms. I will love you. I will die, holding that thought.

The birth certificate scotchtaped to the endpage read in part, Richard Rodgers, born May 18,1990.

Louise's mother possessed a copy, and had read him the name and birthdate over the phone. Now March read this with his own two eyes.

"Dude, glad to see you, come on in," Leroi, aka Sinistah, exclaimed, giving R. a warm hug at the door.

"Leroi," replied R., walking in a bit tentatively, on cat's feet. "I need a dump truck to unload my head now, like the poet said. Heavy stuff going down. Dunno how frisky and loose I'll be, give it a go I guess."

"Dude, whassup? Kimberly got you on the ropes?" Leroi joked, in a friendly way. "Tell Leroi."

"Kimberly's fine," said R. "Other stuff…"

--"Props for your *youtube* songs by the way."

"Studio, atelier, salon, workshop, business. Subject to despondency, thralldom, slavery," R intoned.

"Huh?" declared Leroi.

"Could you repeat what you said?," replied R. snapping out of it.

"Props for your *youtube* songs, they're a hit" replied Leroi.

--"No songs on *youtube*, must be another guy with the same name. Funny, I keep running into identity issues, and now there's music from another Richard Rodgers on *youtube*, it's the age of anonymity and craven hype, my friend, smoke and mirrors, identity theft."

--Leroi started laughing. "No, dude. Not an identity thief, not another Richard Rodgers, your songs. I should know, I'm in the video with you, playing and singing harmonies."

"But how?" R. stuttered, openmouthed. "Could that be? I'm not a video star. I keep my songs to myself, they're my trade secrets," R. joked, self consciously.

"Gotcha," smiled Leroi. "Dude, the party, remember? Your friend with the camera, at the Pike's house. You know, An Evening of Music and Poetry with Richard Rodgers. He videotaped the event. You're famous."

"Famous," joked R. "Right. I didn't know he could do that, make it all public like that. Maybe that's why he's been calling me, haven't gotten back to him yet."

"For all the world to see," teased Leroi. "Dude, you are behind the curve. You're on the internet now, with over 300,000 views."

"Huh?" R. cried.

--"Your friend did a nice job on the editing side, bells and whistles, with dissolves, zooms, fades, cuts. Damn good film editor. In fact so good, I may refer my clients to him. The guy's got celluloid mojo."

"Peter, that rascal. He didn't even tell me. Oh yeah, Peter's an accomplished guy, heads up a film foundation, receives government grants, to develop "underdog" projects, or some such. On a panel with his peers. Peter's made a few short films himself, a nature walk through Muir Woods, if I recall. Also, a short Luis Bunuel biopic, or thereabouts."

"Whatever," Leroi declared. "He did a good job. But the main thing's the music, the performance. Did you realize what a show we put on that night? We were rocking."

"To be honest, after a glass of wine or two, and a cold medicine I was on that night, I do not remember all that much," R. replied. "Tell me."

"Check it out when you get home. Kimberly's got a few cameos. We put over your songs with emotion and style. What's on the menu for tonight?"

"Well," said R. "Have a couple new songs. Keeping up with the history theme. A song about Ben Franklin," replied R.

"Ben Franklin," Leroi replied. "You mean the honky slave owner, big overweight bald guy?"

"Leroi," R. sighed. "Should I take this someplace else?"

"I'm only playing with joo," said Leroi, chuckling. "I'm with you. 300,000 views on *youtube* for a hometown concert. I've never received more than a couple thousand for my own stuff, I'll tell you. Many of my clients are happy with 5,000 views or so. You're doing something right, kid. You received a huge response, and who knows, it's early, online a week or so, could only get better from here," Leroi declared in an encouraging way.

"But how?" R. began.

"Dunno how. Secret Hero turned me onto this. Gave me a call one night, all excited, and whooping. Secret Hero's a *youtube* junkie. Says it helps him stay cool, calm and collected, even at the hospital."

R. closed his eyes, took a breath. "Alright, Ben Franklin. Many people don't know," R. began.

"He owned slaves and dated the slave girls out behind the barn," interjected Leroi.

"Leroi," R laughed, despite himself.

"I'm messin' with you," Leroi confessed. "I don't know."

"I don't know either. But if I'm not mistaken, Ben never owned any slaves. Ben was a Quaker. Yes, it's coming back to me, Ben Franklin was among the first to declare slavery an un-American evil, illegal, and immoral, and advocate for the abolition of slavery."

"And then take the serving girl out behind the barn?" Leroi chided.

"Jeez, are you stuck on a pile of clichés, or malicious gossip, or what?"

"Go ahead," said Leroi. "Tell me."

"Well, speaking of which, plenty going around, I stumbled on an article a few months ago, mentioning that Ben Franklin was a villain and pretender. The rumor was that he belonged to a satanic cult. Also, that he may have been a mass murderer. Apparently, this author on his blog, was citing the story that a score of corpses, about 20 or so, had been discovered under his house, 70 years or so after he died, around 1860. Grossed everybody out, under the famous Ben Franklin's house. The founding father who's on our $100 bill."

"See that, told you," Leroi declared triumphantly.

"Turns out," replied R., with his competitive juices up, "and this libel is all over the internet, that Ben's heirs sold his house not long after his death, and it passed to a succession of owners over the years, one being a medical examiner. The medical examiner had a license to build a morgue in his basement. The bodies are the remains of John and Jane Does, many the victims of violent crimes. The examiner worked with the local police to solve the crimes, and in time, buried the remains. This was over 50 years after Ben was gone. Also, Ben belonged to the Masons, a popular fraternal Order at the time, the pyramid with the eye on top on the dollar bill is a Masonic symbol, standing for liberty and enlightenment."

"Okay," said Leroi, a little disappointed. "An overweight, balding white guy. Why write a song about him?"

"Leroi, ever hear of a lightning rod?" R. queried.

"Sure," said Leroi. "This building has one, by state law probably. Conducts lightning into the ground. Saves buildings from being struck by lightning and burning down. If lightning strikes, no damage."

"Well, Ben Franklin invented the lightning rod."

--"No shit," said Leroi.

--"Way back when, before the U.S. was even a country, when the British boots and foreign soldiers struck fear and loathing into the hearts of the farmers and settlers, Ben was experimenting with electricity."

"You don't say," said Leroi.

"Saved many a colonial barn from going up in blazes due to a lightning strike. You know how fast wood would blaze subject to a lightning hit. It was a big deal, a very big deal."

"Score one for Ben," admitted Leroi. "What else ya got?"

"Ben was revered as a genius in France, where he served as French ambassador, during much of the revolutionary war. Why? The Franklin stove ring a bell? Keeps the colonists warm at night. Ben delivered. Ben designed it to optimize heat conduction and convection. Ben flew a kite with his son one night. Carefully prepared an experiment to demonstrate how lightning conducts electrical current, through a key attached to the kite. Ben helped reveal the secrets of electrical current. He coined terms we use today, everyday terms, like "positive" and "negative" polarity, and "conductor." You know, light, heat, Con Ed, the power utilities. Ben did pioneering work on the phenomena of electricity. There's a saying, he snatched the lightning from the heavens."

"Who knew?" Leroi joked. "The old boy did a few things," Leroi admitted, engagingly.

"Mapped the Gulf current, "added R. "Composed *Poor Richard's Almanac,* a popular read in the colonies. Advocated for daylight savings time, to keep working folks longer in the light. Helped win the Revolutionary War by advocating for the colonies, and convincing France, with his charm, and scientific reputation, that the colonies deserved liberation from the British. If the colonies bore fruit, with the quality of men like Ben, they reasoned, the colonists proved they were worthy, with such leaders, and deserved their independence. The French allied with the colonies. They sent their best general, Lafayette, to fight the British. Lafayette's navy proved decisive in several important battles. Including the final battle of Yorktown, in Virginia. Thus, insuring the colonial victory in the Revolutionary War. Invented a flexible catheter. Advocated for liberal values, and less punitive measures, though they did not call it that then."

"Right on, Ben," exclaimed Leroi. "The little guy on the C-note did that, I'm impressed."

"So, here's my song about Ben," said R. R. picked up his guitar and began strumming.

Ben Franklin invents lightnin' rods,
ol Ben flies a kite,
when lightning strikes what a fright
sparks fly from Ben Franklin's mind.
Ben travels on a ship to France,
ambassador for the colonies,
gets tangled up in many a romance

leaves em smilin' many say, does he.
Debonair, oh so debonair,
who cares if he's overweight? What a head of hair.

Friends with Jefferson, Adams, Hancock too,
got friends in Phili, Washington and Massachu…

Grew up with 15 brothers and sisters,
father scratched and saved to make a home,
Ben wakes, a curious lad,
swims a lake, hills and valleys roams.
You'll find Ben on a $100 bill,
smilin' to this day,
walked the walk and when he stumbled,
ate humble pie all day.
Debonair, oh so debonair,
who cares if he's overweight? What a head of hair.

Saved houses and barns Ben,
roly poly Ben,
Franklin stove keeps his comrades warm at night,
go fly a kite Ben.

After R. completed his song, he exclaimed, "sometimes I feel like a mongrel who's been kicked around too much by the powers-that-be, I want to run away, disappear, away from here."

"Okay," said Leroi.

"Orpheus, the music maker, had his throat cut by a Maenad, a drunken women, who held his hair tight from behind while plunging a sword into his neck. To defend himself, the poet brandished his lyre like a weapon, and sang."

"Okay," repeated Leroi, looking concerned. "To be honest, I've never heard songs like these history songs you do. I got to hand it to you, they're unique. So totally flipping the trend, and going against the current, you know. You speak with authority, you're musical, you're passionate, and intelligent. It gets a person to thinking. You know, totally contra what most musicians are doing. Crazy enough, they may engage and appeal," Leroi continued. "Though that crazy party performance on *youtube,* not many musicians could come across so loosey-goosey, so edgy, and so bright, at once. Props, my man."

"I'm feeling desperate," said R.

"Richard," rejoined Leroi. "Why don't you and Kimberly come over for dinner later this week? Meet my wife Tanya. My daughter Keisha, my five year old. After dinner, we'll let the gals do their thing, and go into my personal studio, kick back, relax, play around, maybe find a groove. What do you say?"

"Maybe," replied R. "Appreciate the invite. I'm going through..."

"Well, we're in the middle of a session, let's find a tempo for Ben Franklin, right?" Leroi pressed on.

"Let's do it," R. said warmly.

Leroi scooted over to the computer, out from the tangle of mikes and wires, beat software at the ready, and together they found a waltzy-y, relaxed tempo for the story of Ben Franklin. R. followed by doing the guide guitar and vocal, a bearable performance for a guide.

"I'll put on the bass and drums per our usual during

the week," Leroi promised, shuffling through R's chords and lyrics, for a moment.

"That's exactly how I did the guitar and vocal," reassured R.

"I'm starting to hear the bass," encouraged Leroi. "I'll handle it. How about you and Kimberly come over Wednesday evening?" offered Leroi, handing R. a CD at the end of the session, with a few bounces. "Who knows, if I get it done by then, we could work on it after dinner."

"Groovy enough," replied R. "So Ben's pretty hot, huh?" teased R.

"Hot enough," agreed Leroi. "After we get through with him, he'll be sizzling," Leroi joked, in promising tones.

"One more thing," said Leroi, discreetly pocketing his fee for the night, and walking R. out to his car. "What do you think of the band name Richard Rodgers feat. Smoke Dat? Smoke Dat, that's me."

"I dunno," said R. "I'm awful with stuff like that."

"Well, get ready. That's the name your friend Peter, or whoever, who shot the video, chose for us on *youtube*. It's not politically correct maybe, but it's got flair."

"Good enough then, I'll leave it to Peter and you. Like I say, I dunno," replied R. "Will I need a manager? I'll need a babysitter, for sure," R. joked.

R. edged his car slowly and carefully out from between the monster dump truck and the black pick up truck. "These trucks," motioned R., rolling his eyes. "It's a game of inches."

"Tell me," said Leroi.

"Lord thank you for this food we eat, it's really good to meet/all together," said Keisha, Leroi's daughter, and "All together," chimed in Leroi, Tanya, and R. on the beat.

Tanya smiled, big spoon in hand, and began dishing out a first helping to Kimberly and R., on either side. "There's catfish," she explained, "and chicken livers, collard greens and cornbread. There's macaroni and cheese and mustard greens. Meatloaf and red beans and rice. Also succotash and sweet potatoes."

"I'm a foster child, never had a father, only the posters of the presidents thumbtacked to my wall, with their little pictures and blurb-y bios, that I rolled up and carried with me, to each new foster home, and put up first thing," R. blurted.

"My goodness," noted Kimberly, "A sumptuous feast, such colorful dishes. How old are you Keisha?" asked Kimberly.

"Five," Keisha replied. "I'm in kindergarten."

"Good for you," replied Kimberly warmly. "Are you learning good things there?"

"Yes," Keisha said primly. "Ms. Johnson will let us spend an extra few minutes at recess, if we do our work, and behave. So that works out for everyone."

Kimberly, R., Tanya and Leroi chuckled. "Good thinking, Keisha," encouraged her father.

"This food is delicious," Kimberly remarked. "Sweet potatoes, umm."

"Thanks," said Tanya. "It's soul food, comfort food for us. Part of our heritage. You know, not all that different than our grandparents ate down south, and their grandparents before them, on the plantations. It's not hardcore though. Pork rinds, hogshead, and chitlins, we pass on that. More like soul food lite," remarked Tanya, passing the sweet potatoes.

R. and Leroi, Keisha and Tanya ate wholeheartedly.

"Richard tells me you're in nursing school Kimberly. How's that going for you?" asked Leroi.

"Nursing school's alright. Study hard, learning a lot," replied Kimberly. "My mother's a nurse, and my father's a doctor, teaching now at the university. Guess I'm following in their footsteps. But I'm a music lover. And in my heart, I'm a 'wild and crazy girl,' Kimberly joked, mimicking the Saturday Nite Live routine. "So Richard and I have much in common," Kimberly concluded, to chuckles.

"How about you?" Kimberly asked Tanya.

"Work for the Social Security Administration," she replied matter-of-factly.

"I'm a flight attendant for *Jet Blue*," Leroi added. "How do you like me now?"

"Really?" said Kimberly.

"Yes, they cut my hours a couple years ago, gives me time to get into the music production biz, it turns out to be a blessing. My life seems fuller with music in the evenings, even if it's often 12 hour days, like with Richard."

"Oh, come on," protested R.

"Only joking," chuckled Leroi. "Keisha's been showing me her music skills lately. Keisha, want to start us off on 'Swing Low' and we'll join in?"

Keisha's eyes sparkled. She was wearing blue pants, and a pink blouse with ruffles, when she stood up.

Swing low sweet chariot,
coming for to carry me home,
swing low sweet chariot,
coming for to carry me home.

I looked over Jordan, what did I see?
coming for to carry me home,
a band of angel's a-coming after me,
coming for to carry me home.

Swing low sweet chariot,
coming for to carry me home,
swing low sweet chariot,
coming for to carry me home.

"Awesome," cried Kimberly.

Keisha's husky, sonorous voice filled the room, and tingled their nerves. Kimberly found it amazing, the voice of this five year old.

"They grow up so fast," Tanya joked.

"Keisha, would you sing us another song?," inquired Leroi, after they had joined in the chorus to "Swing Low Sweet Chariot." The temperature in the room was rising. Keisha blushed, and sang.

Wade in the water,
wade in the water children,
wade in the water,
God's gonna trouble the water.

The table burst into applause. She sang in tune.

"Keisha and I were practicing 'We Are The Children' yesterday. Keisha, want to sing for us, please?" Leroi cajoled pleasingly.

"Oh, Daddy," she sidled over to him, and gave him a hug. "Only if you sing with me, okay?"

"Okay," said Leroi. They sang together.
We are the world, we are the children,
we are the ones who make a brighter day,
so let's start giving.

There's a choice we're making,
we're saving our own lives,
it's true we make a brighter day
just you and me.

"We are all a part of God's great family," Keisha concluded to great applause.

"Come with me," Leroi ordered R., while the gals were busy talking, and Keisha sat on her mother's lap.

R. followed Leroi into his studio. "Do you believe in God?" Leroi asked in a mock stern tone, with laughter in his eyes.

"The heavens," R. replied, straight-faced.

"Jesus?" Leroi asked. "That's okay, a lot of my friends are atheists," he reassured R. playfully.

"Jesus, yes. New dimensions, Jesus goes there."

"Dude, come to church with us Sunday. You'll hear gospel music. Have a feeling this will strike a chord," urged Leroi.

"I'll think about it," said R. "Awesome studio," he

noted, gazing on the array of keyboards, guitars, amps, sound board, and computer gear. "Your daughter's a jewel," said R.

"I know," replied Leroi. "You should have met me 10 years ago, I was doing damage. I feel blessed these days, indeed."

They shared long goodbyes at the door, and Kimberly and R. invited Leroi, Tanya, and of course Keisha, over for dinner at R.'s apartment, in the near future.

"Hi ho, ho ho, it's off to work I go," sang R. good humoredly, sleepy, his bio rhythms not quite adjusted to these early school days subbing. Slowly, driving along, the morning snapped into focus, out from the suburbs, into the rolling hills, rural Connecticut in December with but a few inches of snow on the sides, melting away for the moment in the morning sun.

A steady stream of substitute teaching calls cheered him, and gave him a calling, as it were. A future, a potential, a labor he enjoyed. Buffer also, and escape from the crazy phone call recently from March Nesmith, bringing back his past with a vengeance.

Kimberly encouraged him to check with foster services in Texas, obtain information about his parents, if possible. R. was not inclined to. "I don't remember," and "don't look back" was among his favorite phrases, with regards to his early childhood.

He pulled into the school parking lot, and walked briskly into the main office. He secured Ms. Blashka's lesson plans from her mail box. He noted a few familiar units. An Oscar Wilde play, *The Importance Of Being*

Earnest. Oh yeah, the bunburrying, the naughty repartee, the wicked satire, half of which would be lost on the kids, but, amusing anyway, hopefully. The short story "Rashemon", about multiple perspectives in medieval Japan, touching on a lady's robbery and possible rape, on the highway. Julius Caesar, the will to power, democracy versus the divine rite of kings, Rome rife with omens, mobs, jealousy, conspiracies, not to mention famous battles.

"Mr. Rodgers," he wrote on the board, in large, straight, easy to read letters. In swarmed the kids, first period, Julius Caesar would meet the masses.

R. introduced himself, and took attendance. "Mr. Rodgers, it's a wonderful day in the neighborhood," a young man sang derisively in the back row, the catchphrase from the children's show. R. giggled himself, it was funny.

"Yes," R. laughed expansively. A few laughed back, with him.

"Well, I understand you guys have been reading and discussing Julius Caesar. Ms. Blashka provided us a few speeches she wants us to focus on today. "But before we get down to it, let me ask you, is this a true story or fiction?"

A few hands shot up. A group of 25 or so, many of them larger in stature than he was. Seniors, including perhaps a few football players.

"True story," said Veronica, a lithe student with sandy blonde hair, and a touch of blue mascara on her eyes.

"Mostly fiction," a male student, Cameron, in the

second row begged to differ. "Shakespeare based it on a historical event, but they did not talk like that, anyway."

After glancing at the seating chart, for their names, R. looked around.

"Well, when did the play occur? Anyone?"

"About 50 years before Christ," came a reply.

"Yes," said R. "Shakespeare drew heavily from Plutarch's account, written a couple hundred years after the fact, and itself based on many contemporary accounts."

"Why do we have to study this anyway?" came a bored rejoinder.

"I often ask myself questions like this," R. replied, not dissing him, or blowing him off. "A popular president in America, say his supporters wanted him to be crowned king?"

"We have a democracy," Rory, in the third row, declared dismissively.

"Right," said R. "How about Rome, did they have a democracy?"

No one raised their hand.

"Important background," noted R. "Rome had a democracy over 200 years old, almost as old as our own here in the States. They borrowed their government model from the Greeks, after a series of lousy kings almost ruined them. Into this tradition steps the wildly popular Caesar, conqueror of foreign lands, and permits and encourages his supporters to suggest Caesar be king of Rome."

"Ms. Blashka never mentioned that," a girl in the front row complained.

"Yes, she did, bozo."

"No, she didn't, moron."

R. looked at them, and sighed. "Alrighty then," R. declared histrionically.

"Jim Carrey movie," said another. "That's funny."

"Caesar wanted absolute power," R. continued, pressing home the point.

"Boo," said a male student in the front.

"I'm on the football team. We need strong leaders, our coach says," a huge beefy guy with arms like tree trunks, in the back row exclaimed.

"So you're saying the conspirators have history on their side, and Caesar's violating the law," inquired a brunette in the second row, with glasses, and her hair in a bun. "Hmm. Ms. Blashka emphasized the personal motives, jealousy, and ego, of the conspirators."

"A feature that makes Shakespeare great. The play accommodates multiple views," explained R. "We learn to live with ambivalence, and shades of gray, where government and human rights, power and morals intersect. Remember what happens in the first scene, Flavius and his companions are telling the crowd 'go home,' and tearing down posters of Caesar. What happens to them?"

No one answers.

"The play later mentions only this, 'they are silenced.'"

"Silenced, like dead?" a student inquires. A hush falls in the room.

"Yes, that's the implication," declared R.

"Damn," said another. "So much for human rights.

Maybe Caesar wasn't the victim after all?"

"And maybe," said another, "the conspirators, to a degree anyway, had principles, and cared about their country."

"Alright, turning to the speeches," R. shifted gears. "So far, so good. But could it last?" he wondered. "Anthony's speech at Caesar's funeral. Who'll embrace the opportunity to shine, and impress us with your perspicacity and your articulation, and read to us?"

A lean, athletic guy in the second row raised his hand. "Bryon," said R., with a quick glimpse at the seating chart. He was getting pretty good at this.

Friends, Romans, countrymen, lend me your ears.
I come to bury Caesar, not to praise him.
The evil that men do lives after them;
The good is oft interred with their bones.

"Well read," encouraged R. "Let's get down to it, what is Marc Anthony doing here?"

A few hands shot up. R. selected a gal with broad shoulders and long, brown hair. "He's grieving and he's scheming," she exclaimed.

"Good summary." shot back R. "Explain."

"Caesar was Anthony's mentor, Anthony loved Caesar, and he hates the conspirators. But he cannot say that, they would kill him. So he's biding his time, and intends to incite the crowd, while seeming to play ball with the conspirators. Anthony's walking the razor's edge." Nadia explained.

"Couldn't have said it better myself," R. exclaimed.

"Why don't the conspirators kill Marc Anthony right away, knowing he's Caesar's friend and protege?"

"Why indeed? Anyone?"

"Because the conspirators are afraid the crowd will see them as bloodthirsty. They are afraid of appearing criminal," replied Shane, in the third row. "They have to justify their actions to the people. Caesar wanted to be king, and overthrow Rome's democracy. So, he was assassinated, to preserve the greater good. But Marc Anthony has done nothing wrong. Not yet anyway."

"Correct," said R.

"'Lend me your ears,' that's from a Beatles song, a gal in the second row, remarked.

"Joe Cocker, dumbass," retorted a boy in the third row.

"Octavius and Marc Anthony team up, against Brutus and Cassius, and whip their butts at Phillipi," offered a guy in the back enthusiastically.

"True, Scott," declared R. with a quick glance at the seating chart. "But if they were such enemies, why would Marc Anthony say at Brutus' funeral, 'here lies the noblest Roman of them all?'" R. reminded them. "Food for thought," R. declared, as the bell rang.

"You're a good teacher," Clara declared, while gathering her books to leave. "Our best substitute. Many of them read a newspaper."

"Thank you, Clara," R. responded gratefully. "You made my day." Clara sidled up to the desk. "You're welcome," she said, for a moment giving him a warm, full gaze.

"What else do you do?" she inquired innocently.

"Oh, a thing or two. Have a little band."

"Had a feeling," she exclaimed. "You remind me of someone. But I'm not sure who. Is your band on the internet?"

"I dunno," said R. "I'm told. Look up Richard Rodgers. Let me know," said R. absurdly. It was true, he chose to ignore his *youtube* popularity.

"I stumbled, I saw, I guided," R. murmured, after the students exited. On to Period 2. "Students are the destiny of the community, teachers are their guide."

13

"They don't talk English," Marge lamented, albeit querulously.

"Now, Marge..."

"Well, they don't. I cannot understand them."

"Well, dear, your hearing's a problem. Let's see about that," Dolores Pike nudged gently, soothing the 93 year old.

"And my children do not come around to help me. Where are they?"

"Now that's not true. Josie says you returned from a nice dinner with them yesterday evening, remember?"

"Wasn't that months ago?" retorted Marge peevishly. "I don't always remember." She put her head in her hands and began to weep.

Dolores Pike sighed. Being head nurse for 200 seniors in an assisted living community was hard work.

Dolores opened the top drawer in Marge's little bureau in the hall, and retrieved Marge's hearing aid supplies, placed there by her children.

"Tubes and tips need replacing," Dolores informed Marge briskly. Dolores engaged her patients with a brisk, lively friendliness, and easy smile.

"I cannot hear out of my left ear," repeated Marge a few times, as if Dolores was deaf. Dolores tested the left hearing aid on her own ear. She clicked the tiny volume button, holding it up to her ear. It worked fine. She cycled through to the highest volume. She reinserted the hearing aid into Marge's left ear. "Marge, can you hear my voice?"

Dolores looked at Marge calmly and spoke in an even tone. Hard-of-hearing do not like being shouted at any more than normal hearing folks, Dolores was well aware.

"Nothing," replied Marge, with the piece inserted into her ear. "These things are a pain in the ass."

"Alright, I'll let your children know they should schedule you an appointment with an audiologist. Wax build up again, probably. You haven't been dropping batteries in your ear again have you?" Dolores inquired. A couple months before, an audiologist found a tiny battery in her ear.

"I'm a retired real estate agent," Marge declared. "This is not the happiest time of my life. In fact, it's the pits. I'm always in pain. My hip hurts terribly."

"Dear, we're doing our best. If the pain's a bit much, we have Percocet for rough spells."

"I like you," Marge replied, grabbing Dolore's hand. "The other ones don't talk English."

"Marge, your hearing's the issue. They may speak with an accent."

"Accents," Marge cried victoriously. Dolores noted her symptoms of dementia increasing. "I don't need them," Marge retorted. "I don't want help dressing in the morning," she declared emphatically.

"Are you sure?" Dolores inquired. The eldest, like Marge, in their nineties, strove to maintain their dignity.

"I'll dress myself," Marge re-asserted. "I'm paying too much." Her two arthritic hands, while she fiddled with her hearing aids, resembled claws for a moment.

On her return to the nursing station and staff room, Dolores' phone rang.

"Ms. Dolores Pike?"

"Yes," replied Dolores.

"This is the front desk at Connecticut General hospital. Your husband's been admitted to the hospital, with an arhythmia. He's in Room 309."

"Oh dear, I'll be over directly," click.

"It's life against death, a retrogressive, hardcore negativity, based on a driftwood past, versus a progressive, healing, and I cycle through these phases, dark and light, meanwhile having this metal plate in my head, and numbness in my lower lip, like novacaine," R. confessed to Kimberly, taking off his coat. "Which side will win?" he wondered histrionically.

Kimberly came up and hugged him. "My father's in the hospital, I'm on my way out," she cried, with tears in her eyes. "Mom just called."

"Should I go with you?" R. wondered, alarmed.

"I'll call you," Kimberly replied. "Don't fall apart on me, I need you now," Kimberly exclaimed, and was gone.

"The prognosis is positive," the doctor assured Dolores and Kimberly, at the hospital. "We have him under observation. He seems to be improving. He can go home tomorrow, assuming there's no relapse."

"What happened?" both queried, on edge.

"An arythmia. We'll give him a slightly stronger medication. Exercise in moderation does wonders for this kind of thing. A 20 minute walk every day, for example."

"He used to work out every day at the gym on the exercise bike. But he's stopped going the last couple of months, for some reason," Dolores explained.

"Well, walking may be preferable, the bike may be too high-impact," the doctor explained.

"I'll see to it," Dolores declared firmly. "Won't we, Kimberly?"

"Definitely," Kimberly declared. "We will read him the riot act. Can we see him now?"

"Yes, he's awake and resting," the doctor said. "You know what they say. Doctors make lousy patients. He's tired of us already. You'll be welcome."

Kimberly rushed to hug her father, in his bed. "Oh, daddy," she exclaimed. "Thank God, you're alright." His craggy face, his eagle eyes, looked tired, and his salt-and-pepper hair, streaked with silver, seemed grayer.

"Sweetheart," he hugged her back, firmly. "Sorry about all this," he said wearily, gesturing to the monitors and IVs. "Yesterday I'm lecturing on the history of medicine, and today I'm here. Life's funny that way, isn't it?"

They laughed and cried, and cried and laughed, for a moment.

Three months later.

"I'm freaking out," declared Kimberly.

Kimberly Pike and Britney Steere reunited again,

drove a scenic route, up around the Connecticut Berkshires, Britney's old stomping grounds. About nine months had passed since their last meeting, and much had happened in the interval. Kimberly's relationship with R. was "serious", she assured Britney, and there was his car accident. Britney was chatting about her first year experiences in veterinary school , while they took in the beautiful scenery, and sped along the backroads. The leaves were but buds on the trees, little jutting, pushing green flares. Flowers along the way sprang freshly up, newborn and tentative. Tall, stately oak, graceful hickories, pliant willows, stirred with the promise of a new day. They awoke from winter's slumber, eager, if demur, in the cool breeze, early April. Born again!

In a few weeks, May would hold sway, with its darling buds, and winter would be foaming at the mouth behind them, receding in the rear view mirror. However, the spring breeze reminded them winter was vanquished for the moment, in the circle game.

"How was your drive up?" Britney inquired.

"Why do you live two hours away?," moaned Kimberly impulsively. "I miss you. It feels like ages."

"I know, " Britney agreed. "So busy with school. They pile it on like there's no tomorrow. Earned 9 extra credits last summer, barely have time to notice spring is here. Been holed up with books and exams, too much."

"Like what?" Kimberly asked.

"Pharmacology, general pathology, histology, gross anatomy, large animal surgery, small animal medicine, for starters."

"Yikes. Good for you," cried Kimberly warmly. "By

the way, what's histology?"

"The study of animal tissues, and the form of structures seen under the microscope, either light, electron, or infrared. Also called microscopic anatomy, as opposed to gross anatomy which involves structures that can be observed with the naked eye."

"Sorry I asked," joked Kimberly. "Oh Britney, I'm so proud of you," Kimberly gushed impulsively.

"Tell me about your first year in nursing school," Britney requested.

"Oh, you know. The usual. Studying about infections, and the like. Have this one b-iatch. She gives quizzes rife with material she does not go over in class, or receive mention in the textbook. Refuses to grade on a curve. Half the class struggles to maintain a "C." How do the bad apples get away with it?"

"The powers that be," quoted Britney. "Hold your nose, and get through it.

"I considered filing a complaint," said Kimberly hotly. "She's stressing me out."

"Yeah, hear you. But wouldn't advise it," replied Britney, if sympathetically. "Play the game. Soon you'll be out from under."

"Richard is more upset with her than I am. He hates that she's distressing me."

"Richard. How goes that?"

"Richard. Drives me crazy on occasion, but so interesting. Leads me to new places, shows me new things. Received over a million hits on *youtube*, a brilliant musician," Kimberly asserted with pride. "All kinds of crazy stuff, though. Did I tell you, he's a foster child.

After his car accident, he hired a private detective. In a series of strange coincidences…found out his mother may be dead. Linked to the doctor that performed surgery the night of the accident. But he hesitates to press the matter."

"That's quite a coincidence," responded Britney.

"Yeah. Too weird. We each have our point of origin. Richard's is very tangled. Who knows, maybe that's what impels his creative side, drives his music?"

Each quietly reflected, driving along the windy, twisty roads. Spring was springing around them, infusing the landscape, filling their senses with profusion and color. The Berkshires loomed loftily in the distance.

"I may be gay," Britney volunteered impulsively. "Go to gay bars, anyway. Enjoy the scene."

"What's that like?" said Kimberly, curious.

"Pretty mellow. Enjoy the music."

Did I say too much
am I losing touch,
did I build this ship to wreck?"

"Florence," Kimberly delared. "Richard likes her."

"Oh, I like him already," joked Britney. She swung her chestnut ponytail around, and smiled at Kimberly. "When we came here about a year ago, you were just getting involved with him, remember?"

"Remember."

"How on earth could this doctor be involved?" wondered Britney.

"Well, we trust our private detective. He secured

DNA samples from Richard. Then from Louise's mother in Colorodo. His mother was a musician also. Died in her early twenties. You know Ginny Rose?"

"The rock'n roller?"

"Yes. Richard's mother formed a band with Ginny, and a couple of other girls, way back in the 90s. She died of a drug overdose, apparently."

"Too sad," Britney exclaimed. "Poor Richard."

"Yeah. But what's really weird. I'm scared to tell him. He's got a metal plate in his head. He's recovering from a serious accident. And now all this stuff is going down."

"Yeah. Sounds ripe for therapy," Britney remarked lightly. "Every day, I see wounded animals. Did you know, animal DNA is similar to human DNA?"

"Really. How similar?"

"Well, there's a bit of range and estimation involved. If I recall, for example, chimpanzees somewhere between 75% and 90% overlap with humans. Dogs about 80% overlap with humans. Cats about 85% overlap with humans. Birds maybe 65% overlap with humans. Tiny little birds that weight less than a pound, like the hummingbird, share so much of our DNA. Isn't that amazing?"

"Yes," said Kimberly. "Richard feels a close bond to birds. Wants to be reincarnated a bird, says he."

"There's an owl back at the lab, where I'm interning. So adorable. A barn owl. Flew into a barbed wire fence in the dark, apparently. Neighbor boys found him the next day, all torn up, and barely alive. They brought him in. I'm helping nurse him. A little heartshaped face, we call him Mikey. Hops to me, when I come in. I put water on his feet and beak. They'll only eat live, you know. Hungers for mice."

"Yeah," said Kimberly. "We share a bond."

"The circle of life," Britney chimed in. "Poor little bird. Healing takes time. Me loves the wee Mikey," Britney's Irish brogue slipped out.

They arrived in the park area. They walked down a trail, into the deep underbrush. "The woods are so plush today," Britney breathed, and exhaled deeply.

"Yeah, feel the oxygen," Kimberly agreed, feeling restored, walking the trail, with the birds twittering in the canopy.

"I brought my bird book, remember?" Britney announced, when they reached a picnic table.

"Read me a few," cried Kimberly. "The birds. They fly. They sing."

Britney read a couple excerpts, touching on the warbler and the vireo. Little birds peeked and peered through the branches.

Each drank a bottle of Evian, and slapped away a few mosquitos. The sun was beginning to set. "Time to go," said Britney.

"Let's say a little prayer before we leave," Kimberly proposed. "Sturdy oak, effusive maple, thank you. The mighty shivering trees the birds thrill with song, bless you."

"The meek, patient trees," Britney intoned. "Bless you."

"Blessed beings, thank you for your generous shade, and oxygen, until next time," added Kimberly. "Amen," the girls said together.

14

"Are you sitting down?" March insisted. March and R. were catching up on the case status, any new developments. "I'd highly advise it. No kidding."

--"I remember the last time you told me to sit down. You dropped a bombshell. Is this a bombshell?" said R. nervously.

"Are you sitting down?"

"Yes."

"Well, more like a tremendous piece of good news. A DNA sample test reveals that Sarah Pierce, Louise's mother, is your grandmother."

"Oh, my God," R. exclaimed. "But how…I have a grandmother?"

"Yes," enthused March, "and one more thing."

"What?" R. wondered could possibly follow this. This meant Louise was his mother. She was dead, but he had found his mother.

"Dr. Fairchild is your father."

"No," said R.

"Yes," said March.

"No," said R. adamantly. "March, is this a joke?" R. demanded. He could not process what March Nesmith was telling him.

"Results are conclusive. Dr. Fairchild is your father," March repeated. "I think it's fabulous news."

"Do I have to pay you for this info? If so, could I deduct it from the judgement I win, after I sue you?" R. demanded heatedly.

--"Why?" asked March. "Richard." March sounded disappointed. "It comes with the territory."

"Dunno if I'm joking, March. I'm like Alice in Wonderland at the moment, and you're the Mad Hatter. You're leading me on a strange, strange trip."

"Only it's not an acid trip, it's real. You've found your biological father."

"But how?" R. stuttered.

"I got creative," March offered.

"Tell me," R. demanded.

--"Well, you understand, I did not want to get your hopes up. I scarfed a sample of your DNA at our last office visit. Remember your cup of coffee I carried to the back? Scarfed up your fresh saliva, and transferred this to a swab. Collected a second sample from Louise's mother, during my visit to Colorado. She was glad to give a sample, when I explained the coincidence of the same birthname and birthday, with Louise's disappeared son. She hopes to meet you. She's excited to have a grandson."

"Oh, my God," exclaimed R. "But the doctor, how did you?"

--"That was a tough one. I made a plan. I put the plan into effect," March explained, a bit of pride creeping into his voice.

"You son-of-a-bitch," R. cried. "How?"

"Richard, all out of respect and love. I've grown quite

fond of you over the last few months. You and Kimberly. I feel your pain," March exclaimed.

"Do you know what a giant, insane coincidence this is, if it's true?" R. cried.

"It's true, it's true," March declared. "First, I made an appointment with Dr. Fairchild. Pretended I wanted a face-lift, and chin tuck procedure. That wasn't hard, I do," March joked. "Scheduled an office visit. And then…"

"You scarfed a sample from his coffee cup? Or a cigarette butt?"

"Nope," said March.

"Swabbed sweat off his arm, brushed against him, while he explained the procedure on his computer?"

"Nope," said March. "The office visit yielded zero opportunity. So, at the end, I took a deep breath, and told him the truth."

"What?," queried R.

"Told him the truth, the whole story, how you hired me to be your private eye, how you were upset due to smelling alcohol on his breath, the night of your accident and surgery. How alittle beatwork leads me to a gal named Louise in Texas. How I touched bases with Ginny Rose, and also Louise's mother in Colorado. And leading up to this moment. The insane coincidence, I told him, that "your patient, Dr. Fairchild, who you operated on, may be your son."

"What did he say?" R. demanded.

"He was thunderstruck, I'll tell you. Thunderstruck. The blood seemed to drain out of his face. 'Louise,' he said. 'I could say I haven't thought about her in years,' he told me. 'But that would not be true.' He paused, lost in thought."

"'How crazy is this,' he sighed. "There were tears in his eyes. Then he snapped out of it and said, 'what do you want? You want money?' I don't know if he thought I was trying to extort him. Or worried about what his family would say ...anyway, I reassured him. In my 25 years being in practice, doing detective work, this case takes the cake. I asked him if he would volunteer a DNA sample. He agreed. So I swabbed his inner cheek, placed it safely and securely in a baggie, and now I had two samples, yours and his.

"Amazing," exclaimed R.

"I sent them off to an accredited lab. The kits are available on Amazon for $99. They provide the results online in a week or so after receiving the swabs."

"Are they reliable?"

"Oh yeah. Hundreds of positive reviews on Amazon, about the kits, 99.999% reliable they claim. They say they utilize a more stringent matching process than the FBI, their match requires 16 matching alleles and the FBI requires 13 only for a match."

"Did tears come to his eyes really?," R. demanded to know.

"Tears rolled down his cheeks, no kidding," March assured him. "He's not all bad, you know. He saved your life the night of the crash. Now you've discovered he's your father."

A pregnant pause. R. did not know what to say. His mind was ablaze. He could not compute it.

"Quantum entanglement," R. muttered.

"Huh?" replied March.

--"My God," said R. "Where do we go from here?"

"I told him the good news," March reported, encouragingly. "He wants to meet with you."

"I don't know," R. replied.

"It'll be good for you. Talk to Kimberly. Let's set up a time. I'll pdf you the DNA match report, so you'll see for yourself."

"Well, I got school," R. stalled. "I'll call you tomorrow," R. promised. "And March, you are one hell of a private eye. If I was in the same room with you, I might punch you in the mouth. You're a bastard," R. concluded, signing off.

Later that week R. and Kimberly drove over to the Pike residence for dinner. Dolores prepared peanut chicken, with yams, and an "adventurous" zucchini with garlic sauce. A nice Caesar salad started the meal. Kimberly talked about her classes at nursing school, and R. chatted about his day teaching. Dolores regaled them with tales about the crew at the senior center. Dr. Pike listened attentively, and appeared a bit haggard and drawn.

After dinner, that Kimberly summed up with a hearty "delish" that made all attending chuckle, Dr. Pike invited R. into his study.

--R. took a seat on a plush leather chair, regarding the bookshelves. Contrary to expectations perhaps, there were varied books on the shelf. R. noted the rows of impressive, large medical books. However, there were also Shakespeare, Joseph Conrad, D.H. Lawrence, and Joseph Campbell. R. recalled how intrigued he was by the doctor's taste before his accident. They had talked in the study frequently.

Now a change was occurring. The doctor seemed to have aged substantially, or perhaps his hair turned a bit grayer. He still had a lean, handsome face, and a broad, confidence-inspiring gaze.

"Richard," he started warmly, when they were settled. "How goes your world? Kimberly tells me you are doing well."

R. took a deep breath. He liked Dr. Pike, but this felt a bit like an interview. Well, for Kimberly's sake, "relax," R. admonished his anxious self.

"Going well, sir," he replied forthrightly. "The kids knock me out. What I mean to say is, there are constant surprises, quite often pleasant surprises. They enliven me with their youthful energy," R. enthused.

"Sounds like a good fit," the doctor exclaimed. "Understand you garnered a long term semester assignment, and you'll be doing the whole shebang, lesson plans, assignments, grades. Look out, it's a lot of work," the doctor warned.

"Yes sir," R. agreed meekly.

"After what you've been through," the doctor began. He paused. "Congratulations son, you seem truly on the road to recovery."

"Well, I have a metal plate in my head, and my lower lip on the left side feels like novacaine there constantly," R. confessed, not wanting to blow many smoke rings.

--"Great progress," the doctor declared. "Understand also your songs have received over a million views on *youtube*. Pretty impressive."

"Thank you, sir."

"More importantly, if I may say, you seem to have won my daughter's heart and mind."

"Kimberly," R. began. And faltered.

"Kimberly," her father said, and paused. A connection passed between the two men, a living current.

"I'm hopeful, sir," R. replied meekly. "You know, I have issues. My past…" R.'s voice trailed off.

--"Kimberly's brought me up to date on a few remarkable, recent developments. Your private detective. His revelations."

"Yes," said R. tentatively. "I don't know..."

"Seems to me a pack of blessings lay on your head," the doctor exhorted, in a booming voice.

R. blushed, and made no reply.

"How so?" said R. finally.

--"Well, you've been through a major car accident, and survived with no permanent injuries or disabilities, there's a blessing."

"Yes, sir," agreed R.

"You've found a new career path that seems to suit you temperamentally, emotionally, and creatively, there's a major blessing."

"Um," said R.

"You've found your father, a remarkable event under the circumstances, there's a blessing. And lastly, Kimberly, she wants to be with you, and you with her, there's a blessing."

"Kimberly," R. repeated, letting his silence speak volumes.

"Amen," replied the doctor. "She likens you to a guide, leading her on a great adventure."

"Oh, she leads me, sir," R. assured him. "I'd be a wreck without her."

"Well," Dr. Pike said broadly, "that's the circle of life, the road to recovery. You've been through a dark night of the soul. You've come out though, you've emerged. With a treasure."

--R. felt suddenly more optimistic. It was true, a pack of blessings were on his head.

The men's gaze connected and tears came to R.'s eyes. "Thank you for your kind words and support, sir," R. heard himself say.

"By the way, Dr. Fairchild called me. He wants to meet with you. He wants to thank you for your intervention."

"Really?" said R. in disbelief.

"The door's open, Richard, are you ready to walk through?" Dr. Pike confided, as the two men, the younger, and the older, returned to the dining room, and the ladies.

2nd Party at the Pike Residence featuring Richard Rodgers

"Mediocrity in the workplace, mediocrity in music, R.'s music is the antidote. And he's ours, homegrown," Peter proclaimed.

"Yeah, baby, I'm down with that," Connor enthused, popping another Heineken.

"Moi aussi," chimed Indiana.

Peter recited, "Mon triste coeur bave a la poupe, mon coeur couvert de caporal…" ("my sad heart slobbers at the poop, my heart covered with tobacco spit.")

"Give me another beer or two, and I'm with you,

marching in the streets," Connor groused rousingly.

"O saisons, o chateaux, quelle ame est sans defaults?/ J'ai fait la magique etude du Bonheur, que nul n'elude/o vive lui, chaque fois que chant le coq gaulois. (o seasons, o castles, what soul is without flaws/I carried out the magic study of happiness that no one eludes,oh! may it live long, each time the Gallic cock crows."), Peter recited.

Dolores Pike, ever the mischievous hostess, greeted each and every guest at the door, and handed them a party favor. Each party favor was unique, usually a child's drawing, holdover from Dolores' teaching years. Or, souvenirs from Kimberly's childhood. Kimberly had been a prolific sketcher. "Art is for everyone," she exclaimed.

The Pike living room looked festive, festooned with a homemade banner, An Evening of Music and Poetry at the Pike Residence, featuring Richard Rodgers. Kimberly applied her script to the banner the evening before. Kimberly commuted tipsily between the buffets, chatting with guests, encouraging R., consulting with R. concerning his set list, his cold, that inevitably seemed bound to concert night, despite his conscientious rehearsals, or maybe because of them. She fed him tea with honey at each break, and before and after the show. That did the trick.

R. played the keyboard, also handled the bass and drums from his Yamaha, Leroi played lead guitar beside R. like a pro sideman, alternately relaxed, and striking poses, showboating, deferential, and precise, given R.'s leadership role. Every so often, he switched to saxophone.

The audience was varied, including fruit from Peter's

promo, friends of Connor, Indiana, and R. of course, Kimberly's crowd, the Happy Bridges crew Dolores had enticed with promises of youth, music and culture, not to mention kids who'd heard R.'s music on *youtube* , and wanted in on a happening event. R. recognized a group of his students from teaching in the audience.

"You sure you won't be jealous?" R. queried Kimberly worried before the show.

"Of course not," Kimberly replied, "would not occur to me. I'm not inclined to censor an artist, would never play that role. Break a leg."

"Kimberly," R. said, and got down on his knee. They both had wineglasses in their hand, faces swirling around them. Peter tested his stage lighting, red, blue, yellow. Dolores floated between guests, offering drinks, the convivial host.

"Rise, good sir," commanded Kimberly.

"Kiss, kiss, kiss me love," begged R. "I wouldn't be here without you. I owe it all to you."

Kimberly and R. came together for a moment, the moving center in a movable feast. "I understand it was years ago. She was your friend. I had a friend, Ron, in my callow youth," said Kimberly. "That's life. Don't be afraid of my feelings. Do your art. I really like the song, you know I've heard you sing it. By the way, I relate to it."

"Just so I'm sure you understand, it was a long time ago, and she was only my friend, and she had a mental illness, and I did not have an affair, or a physical relationship with her, you understand, right?"

"Richard you are starting to drive me crazy. Sing

"Late Bloomer," it's a groovy song, people will love it."

Leroi was bopping here and there, checking levels, twirling dials on the amps, tuning his guitar. His wife Tanya and daughter Keisa were talking with Connor and Indiana. Peter was running around, like a chicken without his head, inspecting camera angles, and vantage points.

"How many hits does Richard have on *youtube*?," Connor queried Peter, at one point in the show.

"Over 1.5 million and climbing," Peter responded, with a touch of pride.

Late Bloomer

Her lilting walk, her flashing eyes
she was poetry in motion, my oh my, don't ask why.
She was a late bloomer
fairest flower in all the field
she burned too bright here to endure the real,
she was a late bloomer
always dancing in the rain, behaving like a clown
in her hometown they put her down.

Orphan Annie in the garden
when she acted out she didn't need a pardon.

She was a late bloomer
fairest flower in all the field
she burned too bright here to endure, to feel
she was a late bloomer
crashed her car up in the snow

lost her grip and spun, just a moment, and she was gone...
Child of the universe I miss you so,
child of the universe I miss you, I miss you so.

A big burst of applause. They liked that one. R. launched into his next song.

In Luv With My Therapist

You wanna hear my confessions, will they haunt you? warm breeze, cupid's dart, challenge my dreams, total up my screams, for I'm a gazelle on the run. I'm in luv with my therapist, and I know the price, welcome to my heart. I'm in luv with my therapist, welcome to my heart, admission $50 an hour.

Raise the curtains on my dramas but step lightly. part madonna, part sugar heart, i'll tell you it all, just give me a call, relax I've already paid. I'm in luv with my therapist and I know the price welcome to my heart. I'm in luv with my therapist, welcome to my heart, admission $50 an hour.

She's a cutie from the bottom of a wishing well, says i'm goin' to heaven cause i've already been to hell, I'm happy just to give her it all...I'm in luv with my therapist, I'm in luv with my therapist, I'm in luv with my therapist, I'm in luv with my therapist...

A big burst of applause, a few pumping fists among the kids. "Rock it," someone called.

"Richard's crossed the electrified door, I can feel it in his work," Connor offered, to a friend, CarryAnne. Indiana sauntered up, glass of wine in his hand, "the electrified door, what's that?" he demanded, curious.

"There be treasure, behind the electrified door," Connor posited. "But you've got to take risks, face death, before you win access. Even then, you may die before you can carry it out. R. got out alive, fortunately."

"His car accident, that being his electrified door," Peter piped up, still shooting, video held up to his eye.

"I dunno," said Connor. "The wine is in me, and I am in the wine," he joked. "Beer and wine, actually."

"Though R. wrote many of these songs before his car crash," Indiana added, interested. "My impression, anyway."

"You know, there's the Dionysian, the Apollonian, and the Socratic personality, in the artist. Dionysus, god of wine, drove a chariot of panthers. Do not mess with Dionysus. The young boy-god looks innocent enough, but like wine, offers intoxicating pleasures, adventures, and dangers. The wine-infused body loosing their primal urges, sex, drugs and rock'n roll," Peter narrated.

"Apollonian," he continued. "The god of the sun. The finely woven veil that touches on our wellsprings, through a glass darkly, with class, with artful finesse."

"Socratic. The philosopher-wizard, on a quest for knowledge and understanding. Including science, history. Casting a cool eye on life, on death, on the changing scenery," Peter concluded.

"Why didn't they teach me this in school?" Connor wondered. "Which one is R.?"

"All of them," Indiana joked. "You lost weight," Indiana noted to Connor.

"20 pounds, lean and mean."

"How's the bike?"

"Traded in my Yamaha for a Harley 1200 Custom. That baby's got mojo."

Connor scanned the room with his lively blue eyes. He was tall, broad-shouldered, and looked fierce and formidable, with his mane of red hair and orange beard. He exuded virile confidence, a warrior. He exuded virile confidence, on the face of it, a warrior a la Leif Erickson.

"Who may this be?" he inquired heartily, turning to Peter.

"This is Cindi," Peter said, and introduced his new girl friend. "Peter's told me so much about you," said Cindi with a smile. Cindi was asian.

"The problem with edgy," said Indiana, "or you may call this Dionysian," he responded to Peter pointedly, "is that risktakers and scouts tend to die young. Edges implies falling off possibilities. Striking a balance with powers beyond our control is part of our maturation process. We move from the animalistic and impulsive, to the moderating and reasonable. Look at the '27' club. You know what I'm talking about. Jimi Hendrix, Jim Morrison, Janis Joplin, Kurt Cobain, Amy Winehouse, to name a few. All risktakers who deranged their sense to create memorable music. All died at 27. Weird, isn't it? They broke through boundaries, and paid the price. They 'broke on through to the other side.' They crossed the point of no return."

"On the other hand," responded Connor, "the 'official' art world is full of phonies. Jackson Pollack throws paint on a huge canvas randomly. Whoopee! Sells his paintings for $10 million a piece. Pizza splatter, a drunken guy over at Little Caesar's could do as well."

"Hear you," replied Indiana, munching a brownie baked by his girlfriend Sheena. Smelling suspiciously like grass.

"Jeez, I'm working on the Landry building in downtown Hartford. My drop clothe resembles a Pollack, after a hard day on the job. Where's my $10 million?"

"Rothko is even worse," Indiana retorted. "Draws a blue rectangle. Over a green rectangle. $5 million dollars, for this rat's ass."

"It's an investment, not a painting," Peter concluded.

"Phony," Connor exclaimed. "R.'s music is real. It comes from the wellsprings. I can feel it."

Said Indiana, "I agree."

"Each day I look down from the scaffolding 30 feet or so in the air, on the traffic below. If I make a wrong move I'm dead," asserted Connor. "That is where art comes from. That's what I hear in R.'s music. It's edgy..."

"You dare to criticize our art establishment? Bad Viking! Seriously, interesting, Connor," said Peter. "That takes guts. I suppose there is a parallel. When I film "edgy" and bring a piece of the House of Mystery into the House of Propriety, I feel alive. That's what I do, that's who I am, a recorder."

"Cool," said Indiana. "So long as you realize that "edgy" is a part of life, but not all of life. Seen on a lavatory wall. 'God is dead.' Neitzsche. Then 'Nietzsche is dead.' God. The 27 Club, long may they be remembered, are gone all too soon."

"Well, that too," agreed Connor. "Where's Cindi?"

"Goes without saying," joked Peter. "She's over by

the buffet talking to Ms. Pike." His eyes radiated his new affection. "Asian girls. They bring something new to the table."

"Whatever works for you," Indiana responded, a bit slyly.

"I'm going to acupuncture. Very relaxing, helps even out my moods. Off my antidepressant, finally. Learning how to cook with a wok. I love it," Peter added.

"What happened to your hand?" said Indiana, gesturing to Connor's wrist area.

"Broken glass. An occupational hazard," Connor replied, checking his two bandaged fingers.

"Isn't the night going wonderfully?" Dolores came back with Cindi, shaking their hands warmly, working around Connor's injured fingers. "Richard's so talented."

"It's a way of escape," Peter joked. "He has to."

A couple of nursing students browsed the buffet. "What are these, Ms. Pike?" one asked. "And these?"

"Vegetarian sandwich and wrap, a canapé platter, and tuna on crackers," she laughed. "Kimberly and I prepared some. Guests bring, you know."

"So colorful. Delicious," declared her companion, sampling a canape.

"The cheese and onion mini-muffins are yummy. I'm on a diet," she complained.

"I'm the femme fatale of fandom," Ariane sashayed by, alluring in a red blouse, and denims with little sparklers. "Who wants to sign up and join me, and hundreds, in the *Richard Rodgers Fan Club?"*

"Richard rocks," agreed the two buffet girls, and put

their names down.

Connor sidled over, with Indiana. "With an ambassador like that," he declared, sotto voice to Indiana, "Richard's going places."

R. launched into a history song, "Lady Liberty." Before he did, he made a brief little intro. "When I was back there in my childhood, living in foster homes, I did not have a father or mother. I connected to a poster of the U.S. presidents, with their little oval pix, and little bios. I rolled up the poster, and carried it from foster home to foster home throughout my youth. The Presidents were my father, in a way, and in a way, the Statue of Liberty was my mother."

Torch held high, thorny crown, every seasick woman and manchild,
look around, right on deck, beacon of hope, majestic and mild.
Sayin' "come on come on, come on come on, to our shores.
come on come on, come on, to our shores.
Our lady Liberty.

"I take walks at night. Broad, treelined suburban streets. Deep, majestic night sky, stars glittering like pinheads. Here's "the Cat, The Moon, The Songbird."

Goin' out for a walk,
goin' out, to hear nature talk,
in the blue, blue summer evenings.
The cat, the crazy-as mockingbird,
and the sweet magnolia tree,
the moon and me.

There's action in the trees,
hidden away from you and me.
The cat and I sit on the curb, listen.
The cat, the crazy-as mockingbird,
and the sweet magnolia tree,
the man in the moon and me.

Woodchucks, robins, hedgehogs, and squirrels,
all come to the fountain to drink,
bluejays, cardinals and the little sparrows,
ain't no time to think/pink.

The cat, the crazy-as mockingbird,
and the sweet magnolia tree,
and you, the man in the moon and me.

"Crazy ass mockingbird," a kid yelled.

Two guys on their IPads cruised the *youtube* page. "Over 1,000 comments," one enthused.

"Sounds like a cross between Dylan and Dave Grolz."

"Richard's so awesome, the Illuminati will have to kill him."

Kids were hanging out on the lawns, with bottles of beer or wine, or talking by their cars.

"Steven Tyler's got the best voice in rock'n roll."

"Kurt Cobain was a genius."

"Steven Tyler's old, dude. Arctic Monkeys rock, 'Crawling Back 2 U.'

"No one plays guitar like Jimi Hendrix."

"That's ancient, man. 21 Pilots, 'Heathen' rules. That's what's happenin' now. Make money."

"Lourdes is singin' my life," a girl with purple hair declared. "She's a goddess. Like Lourdes says, 'I don't care.'"

A police car pulled up, siren blaring, red lights flashing. "What's happening here?" a burly police officer inquired.

"Richard Rodgers rocks, he's a cross between Bob Dylan and 21 Pilots," a kid replied.

The police officer scratched his head. Two girls were dancing in the moonlight. He emerged from his car.

Peter came running out, video in hand, encouraging the crowd. "Who knows, you may be in a Richard Rodgers video. Call your friends," he cried.

Wine bottles and beer bottles flew into their backseats, under a cover.

"We're here for a concert, sir. Richard Rodgers is playing. Richard was in a car accident about a year ago. It messed with his head. Now he's a genius."

The officer sighed. "Well, no loitering," he admonished, and drove off.

A tall, thin guy with orange hair, next to his pick up truck, looking wasted, intoned, "our lady Liberty."

15

"Am I a good man?" Dr. Fairchild asked himself, walking to his car, in the church parking lot, on a Sunday afternoon. The sermon touched on pride, Milton's *Paradise Lost*, and the character of Lucifer.

…"say I could repent and could obtain
By act of grace my former state; how soon
Would hight recall high thoughts, how soon unsay
What feigned submission swore; ease would recant
Vows made in pain, as violent and void.
For never can true reconcilement grow
Where wounds of deadly hate have pierced so deep…
Which way I fly is hell; myself am hell."

"The stresses on doctors, surgeons, such as myself, were major. Could anyone doubt that? Each day a knife fight, tearing open, rending, examining, excising the bad, eliminating the negative, hopefully positive surviving, sewing up. Day after day. Blood and guts stuff. The real deal."

--"My wife says I'm a nerd. I'm boring. My younger son says I'm not there for him. He bangs on the drums and keeps me up all night making an infernal racket. No daughter love to mellow this out."

He was feeling sorry for himself.

"Oh, I remember my youth. My stepfather would say 'get me a beer,' when I'd need to talk to him. Call me 'pussy boy' when I wanted to talk to my mother. Took me out into the garage for a chat one evening. Sat me down at his workbench, by the power saw, drills, pliers. Grabbed my shirt suddenly a propos nothing, and said, 'I could kill you.'"

"The stepfather from hell. And my mother let him. When I mentioned he grabbed my throat she got angry, blamed me. 'I don't believe it,' she cried. 'You must have set him off.'"

He thought back on his youth, his days with Louise and the bands. He lacked musical talent but loved being around music. It reminded him of his father, his true father.

When Louise died, he was shocked. They had only slept together once. He found out when one of the other girls came around requesting a script for Quaaludes. Their band had broken up. Louise had overdosed on booze and pills.

--Shocking. He felt miserable about it. Such a wild kid, and sweet.

--He kept his nose to the grindstone. He wanted to help people. He wanted to be in control. Finished up his residency. No more messing around with female rock'n rollers. Surgeon, he was.

He had received a few warning signs, a few red flags. His drinking grew gradually. A social drinker from his college days, he morphed into a problem drinker. His wife's constant berating did not help alleviate his negative tendencies. Where were his outlets, after a hard day saving lives? Every day he saved lives. He provided well for his family. They lived with silk designer sheets on their beds. And still he felt unloved, under-appreciated, misunderstood.

Now this new kid in town. Complaints to the Connecticut State Board of Health. This one about drinking particularly disturbing, backed up by a nurse.

It was true, he had a problem. He admitted it.

Now a private detective calls and says, "this young man is your son." Would send over DNA proof.

Who would believe it? It was crazy. But DNA does not lie.

The pieces of the puzzle began to fall into place.

He needed help. But he had curbed his drinking habits. No more drinking on the job.

His son did him a favor.

Oddly enough, he was looking forward to meeting him. If this broke up his marriage, so be it.

At a charity benefit, a woman commented to Dr. Fairchild's wife, noting her huge rock of a diamond. "You must be very happy. I've been wanting to get married seven years or more now, but I can't find a person to love me."

Ms. Fairchild replied, and he had overheard her. "Dear, you're wrong, I'm afraid. I have this ring instead of being happy. He rarely talks to me. He gives me rings and things to keep me quiet in the marriage. I wanted communication, trust, and intimacy, but I got detoured by diamonds."

"Lacks communication? She has a larger corpus callosum, the bridge of nerve tissue that connects the left and right hemisphere in the brain. Of course. Could she crack open a patient's chest in 30 seconds, navigate down, and cauterize a bruised badboy liver, fresh from a car crash," he countered savagely, queried vehemently, but to himself.

R.'s car was in the shop. They drove Kimberly's car, Kimberly at the wheel. A momentous occasion held them both in thrall, in nervous anticipation. R. was going to meet his father.

"I don't want your father to leave us," her mother said to Kimberly the night before, in a blue tone. "Often women will cling and cling to the last shred of life, til they are decrepit and corrupted. Men on the other hand, like your father anyway, are like the Roman generals, they will fall on their sword rather than endure the inevitable, irrevocable indignities." Kimberly felt the inherent sadness gnawing at the edges, and was determined that this important meeting would turn out well.

"We are such tender, fragile vessels at times, carrying the current life," she sighed, a propos of nothing.

"When root systems aren't that deep, trees will fall down, topple in inclement weather, that is the danger lacking strong roots," responded R.

"Come on, Richard," Kimberly encouraged. "Let's dwell on a few recent positives, shall we? You've joined the Car Crash Survivors online website group blog, right?"

"Yes. I read their stories, interact on occasion. There's

Amelia, who broke an arm, and both her legs, driving home drunk on her 17th birthday, from her birthday party, at a friend's. She'll be in a wheelchair for a year, at the very least. There's Dallas, who broke his neck in a high velocity crash on the freeway, a truck driver on his cellphone crossed into his lane, and sent him hurtling over the median, where he got smacked again by a hapless civilian driving her kid home from school. No word on the other kid, in the second car. These horrors happen every day."

"It's grueling and heartbreaking," Kimberly responded.

"Expressing, sometimes with humor, gallows humor, picking up the pieces of their broken lives," R. replied heatedly.

"Well, many of them are young, right? Chances are they will recover," Kimberly consoled and encouraged. "Look how lucky you are. Death nearly took you. But you are back, stronger than ever."

--"You're right. Many of them are teenagers. Hadn't thought of that. They will recover," R. agreed.

--"You're back. In touch with your therapist. You like her, right?" said Kimberly.

"She's excellent," R. agreed. "Empathic, helpful, with a pragmatic bent. Encourages me to take one step forward each day. Even baby steps are encouraged. Got me writing down my dreams. Taking long walks, and monitoring the event with Fitbit. Stuff like that."

"You're acing your long term sub assignment, they want you for summer school now. You've got a rave review from the principal. You successfully completed your Ed course certification, and may apply for a permanent teaching position in the coming school year. That's terrific, right?"

"Yes. I enjoy teaching."

"Not to mention your music. Over 25 million views on *youtube,* wow."

"Oh that. That's due to Peter mostly. He's got serious video skills," R. protested modestly.

"Nonsense, Richard. I heard from March Nesmith yesterday, our talented private eye. I've been waiting to tell you, a surprise. Ready for this? Ginny Rose and March are in touch."

"The rock star?" inquired R.

"She wants to meet you. She's heard your music on *youtube.* She wants you to be her opening act when she tours Connecticut later this summer."

"Are you kidding?' R. responded calmly. "But she doesn't know me."

"Time'll tell," Kimberly responded, appreciatively, laughing. "You're making waves," she ventured, excitedly.

"Now we're going to a sit-down, father meets son," R. said morosely.

--"Like negotiating with the U.N., negotiating with you on this matter. Refuse to meet with him at his house. Refuse to meet with him at my parent's house. They would have been gracious hosts, you know."

--"The U.N., the Hague, whatever. My God Kimberly, I'm anxious, I have palpitations," R. explained.

"Of course you do," replied Kimberly, patiently. "That's only natural. Think of it Richard. You are meeting your father."

"Well, how do I overcome them, the trepidations?"

"With hugs," Kimberly replied confidently.

She changed lanes, pulled over onto the shoulder, and screeched to a halt. "Richard, sweetheart." The seating was a little awkward. But not so much so. She clasped his hand and placed it on her heart. "Feel my heart beat," said Kimberly.

"Yes," responded R. "That's our life together," placing her hand on his heart. "Beautiful together." They held each other, heads buried in each other's shoulder for a moment.

"Before we get a ticket," Kimberly cried. "Let's get this meeting over with already."

--R. realized dimly this meeting was an opportunity to relieve himself of an oppressive mythology. Like throwing an iron mask over a cliff.

"'I'll take you to church,' Leroi, aka Sinistah, told me at dinner, not long ago, remember? Maybe I have to learn to forgive."

--"Forgive and forget. Stay on the sunny side. Remember the positive," Kimberly responded. "Don't look a gift horse in the mouth."

--A few minutes later, R. introduced Kimberly to Dr. Fairchild, and did look a gift horse in the mouth. The doctor had pearly white teeth.

"You called me a 'deadhead'," R. accused abruptly.

--"Kids, I'm a human being. Remember, we were talking about music, rock'n roll. You were mentioning bands you enjoyed, Nirvana, 21 Pilots, Bob Dylan, the Grateful Dead. I mentioned I liked the Dead also. I shouldn't have said 'deadhead' when I was examining a car crash survivor. I apologize. But it was in that context."

--"I smelled alcohol on your breath the night you performed surgery on me," R. continued, looking flushed and upset.

--Dr. Fairchild sighed. "It's not easy being a surgeon. There are enormous pressures on me. My son, Nolan aka Ethan, a high school senior, is in a rock'n roll band, and keeps me up many nights banging on the drums. I've got problems. I've got issues. I confess. I'm glad you came along and made that complaint to the State Board. I needed that. I'm taking a good, long, hard look in the mirror. Though I honestly feel a few, it never affected my surgery or injured my patients. It's not a good thing. I'm working on it. No more drinking on the job. Period."

--Dr. Fairchild sat across from R., clearly moved to meet him. His eyes seemed filled to the brim with emotion, and regret.

--"I carry a burden of guilt," he continued. "I don't know if I can ever make this up to you. Fate's brought us together. There are wheels turning within wheels."

Dr. Fairchild looked over at R. expectantly. R. had not expected this, an emotional Dr. Fairchild. His oppressive mythology took a back seat, this was a human episode.

"My son," Dr. Fairchild got down on his knees, and clasped R.'s hand.

--R. remained stonefaced in the moment, a bit taken aback.

"Richard, my son," Dr. Fairchild repeated, and squeezed his hand.

Kimberly leaned towards the two of them, the compassionate witness, the glue, and reached out, and squeezed both of their hands. "Father and son," she exhaled explosively. The two men relaxed, and let it be.

"A friend of mine wrote a song that comes to my lips at the moment," R. declared, as they drove the backroads, towards town. "At the end of the evening, there's just the one and only you."

"Comes with the territory," responded Kimberly. "Yes, and they looked around for a very long time, and learned today what many will spend their whole lives learning."

Walking from the medical center rotunda, arm linked to arm with Kimberly, Kimberly declared, "that wasn't so bad."

"Like pulling teeth," R. joked. "Or brain surgery."

"Cmon, Richard," Kimberly egged him on. "You can do better than that."

She was so catlike and ubiquitous. Her green eyes shone in the sun. "Lately it occurs to me, Kimberly," R. pressed lightly on her arm, and turned his liquid eyes to her, "what a hell of a detour I've been on."

Later, back home, R. was reading and grading papers from school. "Maybe next summer for Thailand, then?" R. queried, out of the blue.

"Maybe next summer. We'll save up. Saving the Chinese cypress tree is important."

"Yes," responded R. "This student paper reminds me of us," R. said provocatively.

"Read it," Kimberly dared.

Embarrassment

"My most embarrassing moment that happened was my first date.

It all began on a Saturday night at this party up in Los A- hills. Anyway, I was just cruising around in my old beat-up Ford when I noticed what looked like a rave party at this two story house. So I pulled up to the curb, cut the engine, and walked in. I hardly knew anyone but I did my best to blend in with the crowd. It was not until the slow music started that things began to change for me. Her name was Nicole and from that first dance with her until the end of the night, I spent talking with her. Some of the interesting facts I learned about her, she was 16, a sophomore in high school, and quite intelligent. At the end of the party, about three in the morning, I offered her a ride home, naturally she accepted. But I did not get home until seven the next morning because I was again out cruising around.

Lucky for me my parents are heavy sleepers, and did not hear me come in. As soon as I got in, I hit the sack. I did not bother getting up until noon because I was dead tired from the night before. Once up and moving around, I decided to give Nicole a call. After deciding what I was going to talk to her about, I dialed her number. It was rather easy talking to her, we talked for about two hours. We talked about politics and how the government should take care of environmental problems, and what to do about them. Finally, after all the talk, I got up the nerve to ask her out. She said "yes", to my surprise.

At the sound of this I was ecstatic, but still calm and

cool. I set the time and place at 6 p.m. at the Century Cinema in K--. I did not offer her a ride, because she lived practically across the street from the movie theater. Anyway, I arrived around 5 p.m. and played video games to work off the nervous edge. In fact, I got so involved in the game that I forgot that I was waiting for Nicole. And because of this she had to pay her own way in. This was nothing compared to the movie we saw. The name of the movie was *Dead Calm* and I never felt like such a fool before in my life. If you want to impress a girl do not take her to see a horror movie. Even though she said she liked the movie, I could see the real truth. And that was that she hated it, to say the least.

That night was the last time I heard from her. Because each time I called, she never answered, or she would pretend that she was someone else, and say that Nicole would return my call later. So I learned one important lesson from this experience. That is if I ever want to have a lasting relationship I am not going to take a date to a horror movie, at least not on the first date."

"My accident is a kind of horror movie and you're my date," R. said lightly.

-Kimberly thought about this. "Silly," she replied. "You're like the seaman who faces the dragon and defeats the dragon, to win the golden fleece, and return home the hero. Your story is about redemption. Salvation."

Epilogue

The mike screeched. EH!!!

R. went on to open for Ginny Rose later that summer. Before each performance, in front of the audience, he would confess. "Surgeon's son. See my scars. I'm an outlier."

He would go on to play songs like "Late Bloomer", "In Luv With My Therapist", "Bedroom Eyes,", dedicated to Kimberly, and the history songs, such as "Jefferson's Expedition," and "Tom Paine." "We love you" would float every so often from the audience. Kimberly, or Ariane, or who knows who. R. never did discover who was so kind, when he did not deserve this, and did not want to know.

Later in the tour, Ginny Rose began introducing R. as the "miracle boy," or "the gifted son of my dear former bandmate Louise, who left this world too early."

"Karma's a bitch," Ginny roared.

www.ingramcontent.com/pod-product-compliance
Lightning Source LLC
LaVergne TN
LVHW091039080826
845145LV00002B/552

9780974468686